'You're u

'I've seen you ... ur heads togethe...

'Was it so o... ...an asked in a small voice.

Simon smiled. 'You were totally transparent—to me at any rate.'

Hannah swallowed. 'Sara and I had a bet on with each other. She bet me that I couldn't get a second date with you. She said you only ever took girls out once.'

Kids. . .one of life's joys, one of life's treasures.

Kisses. . .of warmth, kisses of passion, kisses from mothers and kisses from lovers.

In *Kids & Kisses*. . .every story has it all.

Margaret Barker pursued a variety of interesting careers before she became a full-time author. Besides holding a BA degree in French and Linguistics, she is a Licentiate of the Royal Academy of Music, a State Registered Nurse and a qualified teacher. Happily married, she has two sons, a daughter, and an increasing number of grandchildren. She lives with her husband in a sixteenth-century thatched house near the East Anglian coast.

Recent titles by the same author:

LAKESIDE HOSPITAL
THE DOCTOR'S DAUGHTER
SURGEON'S DILEMMA

IMPOSSIBLE SECRET

BY
MARGARET BARKER

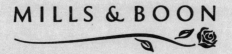

MILLS & BOON

*All the characters in this book have no existence outside the imagina-
tion of the author, and have no relation whatsoever to anyone bearing
the same name or names. They are not even distantly inspired by any
individual known or unknown to the author, and all the incidents are
pure invention.*

*MILLS & BOON, the Rose Device and
LOVE ON CALL are trademarks of the publisher.
Harlequin Mills & Boon Limited,
Eton House, 18-24 Paradise Road, Richmond, Surrey TW9 1SR
This edition published by arrangement with Harlequin Enterprises B.V.*

© Margaret Barker 1995

ISBN 0 263 79092 4

*Set in Times 10 on 12 pt. by
Rowland Phototypesetting Limited
Bury St Edmunds, Suffolk*

03-9506-44462

Made and printed in Great Britain

CHAPTER ONE

HANNAH smiled gratefully as she accepted a cup of tea from the outpatients staff nurse. The afternoon clinic had been open for more than an hour and she was still working her way through two lists of patients instead of one. This wasn't how she'd envisaged her first day as senior registrar in obstetrics and gynae-cology at Moortown General Hospital. She was thinking that she'd like to give the inconsiderate consultant who hadn't yet deigned to turn up a piece of her mind!

'Still no word from Mr Delaware, Staff Nurse?' she asked, between sips of the hot, stewed, but infinitely reviving liquid.

Rona Phillips looked up from replacing the sheet on the examination couch.

'No, Dr Morgan. He's not usually late for his outpatient sessions. He must have got held up somewhere.'

'Then why doesn't he phone?'

'I can't imagine.'

Staff Nurse Phillips glanced briefly in the mirror above the couch as she adjusted her white Sister Dora cap with the broad blue band denoting her qualified status, pushing the wisps of blonde hair away from her forehead. 'He wouldn't dream of being late, if he could help it. I mean, he's always so considerate with us. I never met anybody so——' she paused, as if searching for the right words '—wonderful to work for. We all adore him. But, at the same time, he's got a reputation for having a mind of his own. Doesn't like people breathing down his neck, terribly independent; he's definitely the boss around here and nobody questions what he does.'

'Well, I certainly will!'

Hannah clattered the cup on to the saucer and picked up the notes for the next patient as she thought to herself that she'd met doctors like this Simon Delaware before. Men who could charm the birds from the trees so long as they got their own way in their own little kingdom. And the annoying thing was that the people who worked for them usually fell for their extrovert charm.

She'd learned the hard way to be wary of charming men. There had been the senior surgical registrar at St Teresa's who'd had the nurses eating out of his hand while he offloaded as much of his own work as he could on to Hannah. But being young and anxious to please she'd gone along with it at first, until the strain of exhaustion had become too much for her and she'd given him a piece of her mind. She wasn't going to let that happen again. . .oh, no!

She glanced at the case-notes of the next patient. In the few hours she'd been here, she hadn't had time to work out the Moortown General computer system, so she was glad she'd got paper back-up to help with case-histories.

It had been a hectic week, starting with a phone call on Monday morning informing her that the first-choice candidate for the post of senior registrar at Moortown General had dropped out at the last minute and, as she was second choice, would she like to take up the appointment immediately?

Wouldn't she just! She had been living on a high as she requested special permission to leave St Teresa's Hospital in London. She'd been happy there—first in the medical school, then working post-registration until she was appointed junior registrar. But she'd known that it would be more difficult to climb the professional ladder in the hospital where she'd trained. So she'd applied for a more senior post at Moortown General in Yorkshire, near to where her retired parents were living. She'd been aware that she was just one of many candidates and had been thrilled when she was called back for a second interview on the shortlist, after which she was disappointed when she didn't get the job. So the last-minute phone call, out of the blue, had been a complete shot in the arm.

She'd handed over her job at St Teresa's during Tuesday and Wednesday, packed up her belongings from the tiny North London flat, and set off at the crack of dawn on Thursday to drive north in her ancient Ford Fiesta. She had a brief reunion with her parents at their farm over in Lammendale, during which she was able to off-load most of her heavier possessions and reassure her mum and dad that she would go over to see them as often as her medical duties would permit, and by early evening she had been settling in to her bed-sitting-room in the medical residents' quarters at Moortown General and trying to stay awake long enough to read through the lengthy medical notes her predecessor had prepared for her.

It was now Friday afternoon and her initial euphoria was beginning to evaporate as she forced herself to give all her attention to the job.

'Shall I get the next patient in, Dr Morgan, or. . .?'
The staff nurse's voice trailed away as the door
opened.

Hannah eyed the newcomer warily. He had an
instantaneously commanding presence, oozing confidence from every pore, even though dressed in the
most casual clothes, albeit obvious designer labels:
light brown, cavalry twill trousers, neatly pressed but
decidedly dusty where they merged with the expensive-
looking, soft brown leather shoes, a leather jacket and
an open-necked linen shirt, with dark hairs filling the
space. Shorter dark hairs showed in a hazy stubble
around his determined, cleft-in-the-middle chin, giving
him the appearance of a film director, a show-biz per-
sonality or at the very least an out-of-work actor.

He looked round the consulting-room and smiled at
Staff Nurse Phillips, whose cheeks turned a deeper
pink as she smiled back, her hand moving once more
up to her cap, as if to reassure herself that she was
looking her best in front of her obviously adored boss.

'Mr Delaware,' Rona Phillips said. 'I'm so glad
you've arrived. We were worried about you.'

The consultant's bright charming smile broadened,
to reveal strong white even teeth.

'No need to worry, Rona. I'm here now.' He turned
and flashed the smile in Hannah's direction. 'And you
must be Hannah Morgan.' He held out his hand
towards her. 'Simon Delaware.'

Hannah remained deliberately stony-faced, but
decided it would be too obviously churlish not to shake
hands with her new boss.

Her fingers were briefly gripped before Simon

Delaware sat down in the patients' chair, his dark eyes scrutinising her face.

'Any problems?' he asked in a deep, authoritative tone.

'Nothing I couldn't handle,' Hannah replied. She paused. Should she start as she meant to go on? If she didn't, this inconsiderate boss would think she was a push-over. 'Apart from having two lists to cope with,' she added, her voice steely calm.

She faced him with a studiously bland expression. His eyes didn't even flicker, she noticed. They were brown, with a dark, enigmatic expression that told her nothing about what first impressions he was forming about her. But she could see she hadn't got through to him. He seemed not to notice her smouldering anger.

'Well, don't let me keep you from your work, Dr Morgan,' he said evenly as he stood up. 'We'll talk later, at the end of the clinic. Mustn't keep the patients waiting.'

Hannah took a deep breath. 'Did you have problems getting here today, Mr Delaware?'

He turned as he reached the door. 'I got held up on the motorway. There was a car crash. One of the drivers was badly injured; he's in Casualty at the moment. His wife went into premature labour and I was just in time to deliver her little boy. The police called the hospital, but obviously you didn't get my message. I've admitted the baby to the prem unit. Go up and see him when you finish here and check out the mother in Obstetrics. Our junior registrar, Sara Clarkson, is up there.'

Hannah could feel herself shrinking into the back of the chair.

'Mr Delaware. . .' she began, but the door was already closing behind him.

She felt very small, but at the same time there was something decidedly off-hand about her new boss. He seemed to have taken an instant dislike to her, which was understandable, considering the inimical vibes she'd given out when he arrived!

Staff Nurse Phillips was watching her carefully.

'I think I put my foot in it there, didn't I?' Hannah said, with a wry grin.

The staff nurse smiled. 'You weren't to know what Mr Delaware was up to. He's a bit of a dark horse, and nothing he did would surprise me.'

'How do you mean?'

She hesitated. 'Well, nobody seems to know anything about him. . .where he came from. . .if he's got any family—all that sort of thing. He's absolutely charming but nobody ever really finds out what makes him tick. Rumour has it that——'

'We'd better get on!' Hannah broke in quickly. Whatever the rumours were, it was no concern of hers. She wasn't the least bit interested. . .well, maybe just the normal human curiosity, but she shouldn't waste her valuable professional time on such trivia. Maybe in her off-duty she'd have a chat with someone in the know.

Staff Nurse Phillips brought in the next patient.

For the next hour Hannah was fully occupied with internal examinations, ultrasound scans, checking on weight, nutrition and arrangements for impending confinements. Her deep interest in the fascinating world of obstetrics drove away the tiredness she had been feeling earlier. There was only one more patient to see and then she would be able to go up to Nightingale Wing to familiarise herself with the obstetrics and gynaecology department and check on the prem that Mr Delaware had delivered at the scene of the crash.

As soon as her final patient came in, Hannah could see there was something wrong.

'Sit down, Mrs Bewley. How are you feeling? Only another three weeks to go, haven't you?'

Even as she spoke Hannah was thinking that they would be lucky to take this pregnancy to full-term. The extreme puffiness of the patient's face and hands was immediate cause for concern.

'I've got this awful headache, Doctor. Had it for days and it just won't go away. And the morning sickness gets worse. I thought it was supposed to get better as you went along. I felt so bad I haven't had the energy to come for the last couple of appointments or so.'

Hannah felt it was too late at this stage to impress upon her patient the importance of regular check-ups. She glanced briefly at the notes: Pamela Bewley, age twenty-five, first pregnancy. Last check-up at twenty weeks. It was obvious that this patient had somehow managed to slip through the safety net and avoid ante-natal care during the previous seventeen weeks. Someone should have contacted her. She decided she would have to make enquiries about the antenatal check-up system here.

'I'm sorry you're not feeling well, Mrs Bewley. I'll take a look at you and see what I can do to help.'

Staff Nurse Phillips helped Hannah to ease the patient on to the examination couch. Between them they ran through the necessary tests.

Hannah was apprehensive as she considered the

results: raised blood pressure, protein in the urine, large weight gain. She made a note of the extreme puffiness of her patient's hands and face, the morning sickness late in pregnancy and the constant headache.

'Could you give me something for the headache, Doctor, and something to stop my eyes going all funny? This morning it was like lights flashing all the time; that's really why Dave, my husband, told me I ought to make the effort to come in and see you. I didn't feel like it, but. . .'

'It's a good thing you did come in, Mrs Bewley. We've got one or two problems here, so I'm going to have to keep you in till we've sorted things out.'

'I don't like hospitals!'

'It's the best place for you and your unborn baby at the moment,' Hannah said, her eyes riveted to the screen of the ultrasound scan.

There were definite signs of foetal distress and that, coupled with the fact that her patient had all the signs and symptoms of the dangerous condition known as pre-eclampsia, meant that Hannah would have to move quickly.

She decided that this was not the time to explain the dangers to her patient. A woman who said she didn't like hospitals would become too frightened by what might happen to her and the baby if she developed eclampsia, with its seizures that sometimes led to coma, and which could result in the deaths of both mother and baby.

Speaking quietly to Staff Nurse Phillips, so as not to alarm Mrs Bewley, Hannah asked her to arrange the immediate admission of her patient to Nightingale Wing, before picking up the internal phone to speak

to Mr Delaware. Always best to inform the boss that
he had a new patient.

'So you've diagnosed pre-eclampsia?' Simon
Delaware's voice was professionally calm. 'I'd like to
take a look myself.'

The consultant was in her room in seconds, talking
soothingly to the patient, checking over the signs and
symptoms, before agreeing with Hannah that Mrs
Bewley should be admitted.

'Set up Delivery Room Four. We may have to
induce,' he said to the staff nurse, before turning back
to the patient and taking hold of her hand as he sat
down on a chair beside her.

'We may have to bring your baby along early, Mrs
Bewley. It's the best thing for the baby and for you.'

Hannah noticed the adoring expression in the
patient's eyes as she looked up at her consultant, hanging on his every soothing word. He could charm the
staff and he could charm the patients, which was no
bad thing. And the sympathy he was showing to this
patient seemed absolutely genuine, whereas she
couldn't be sure about the charmingly courteous
manner that had the nursing staff scuttling to obey his
every whim.

'To be honest, it'll be a relief, Doctor,' Mrs Bewley
said. 'I'm past caring any more. Just so long as this
headache goes away. . .'

The trolley had arrived and Simon Delaware stayed
long enough to see his patient comfortably on board.
With Staff Nurse and porter in attendance she was
wheeled off down the corridor.

As Hannah prepared to follow the consultant said,
'I'll be along in a couple of minutes, Dr Morgan. Set

up an intravenous drip through which we can pass the Oxytocin and get things moving. The sooner we get that little fellow out, the better. If there are any problems I'll do a Caesarean. Did you tell Mrs Bewley it's a boy?' he asked, his eyes running over the brief notes Hannah had made as she had monitored the foetus on the screen and noticed the obvious appendage.

'She didn't ask, sir.' Hannah swallowed. The 'sir' had just sort of slipped out. She'd planned not to be too deferential to her new boss, but there was something in his manner that overawed her. 'And I didn't want her to become too attached at this stage. . .just in case. . . Well, I mean. . .'

Simon Delaware nodded. There was no need for words. They both knew that this birth was going to be unusually difficult, and even with all the latest technology and skill there were sometimes unavoidable fatalities.

'We'd better get Mrs Bewley's husband in,' the consultant said. 'He's a nervous type, but I know his wife will want him to be here. I'll ask my secretary to telephone him. We've got his work number down here in the notes. I'll take them through to my room, if I may.'

'Of course.' Hannah watched as her boss gathered up the notes. He was certainly extremely easy to work with—so far! She was already regretting her initial icy reaction to his unavoidable delay. But she wasn't to have known he'd got a legitimate excuse.

Gathering up her stethoscope and the small bag containing some of her personal things, she made her way out into the corridor. As she hurried along her thoughts centred on her patient. If only she'd made the effort to come in for her antenatal checks! The signs of pre-eclampsia would have been picked up much earlier, the mother wouldn't have suffered so much and the potential damage to the foetus would have been avoided.

A staff nurse was sitting at the nurses' station which was immediately through the swing doors of Nightingale Wing. She looked up and smiled as Hannah walked through.

'Can I help you?'

'I'm Hannah Morgan. I. . .'

'Ah, yes, Dr Morgan. Sister Gregson's expecting you in her office. I'll show you in.'

The nurse was turning away to move towards a door at the back of the nurses' station and Hannah noticed a sign hanging beside the door.

'"Calm staff produce calm mothers who produce calm babies,"' she read out. 'That's very true.'

The staff nurse smiled. 'Sister Gregson's motto,' she explained quietly. 'We all have to conform to it. Sister insists that unflappability is of paramount importance in her staff. She's ruled the roost here for the past twelve years and it certainly seems to work. With the nurses, it goes without saying. One sign of hysteria from any one of us and we get a warning; a second show of nervous excitability and we're transferred elsewhere.'

The staff nurse tapped on the door before opening it, then Hannah saw a diminutive woman of about fifty sitting at a desk.

'Sister Gregson, I'm Hannah Morgan. I'm on my way to set up the IV on the pre-eclampsia patient. Mr Delaware said. . .'

'Mr Delaware has already telephoned me, so I've

asked Dr Sara Clarkson to go ahead with it. No need
to flap, Doctor. We've had pre-eclampsia cases before
on Nightingale. Now, why don't you come and have
a cup of tea to revive you after your long session in
Outpatients. A weary doctor is no good to the patients.
Dr Clarkson and two of my experienced staff nurses
are with Mrs Bewley. Take five minutes off before you
join them, Doctor.'

Hannah had the distinct impression that Sister
Gregson wasn't a woman to be trifled with. And the
thought of a five-minute break was most appealing. If
Dr Clarkson had set up the IV there was nothing more
they could do until the start of Mrs Bewley's uterine
contractions.

Sister Gregson served tea from a rose-painted teapot
into bone china cups and saucers. Hannah took a sip;
there was nothing stewed about this fresh brew of Earl
Grey with a slice of lemon. Just how she liked it, but
rarely found the time to produce.

'How is the prem that Mr Delaware delivered this
afternoon?' Hannah asked.

Sister Gregson smoothed an escaping lock of grey-
ing hair that looked as if it had once been a vivid
auburn back into the folds of her complicated stiff
white cap.

'We're nursing him in an incubator, of course—three
pounds eight ounces. Not a bad weight at thirty-two
weeks. What a stroke of luck that Mr Delaware happened to be near the scene of the crash! The father
has just been admitted to Orthopaedics—fractured
femur and suspected internal injuries—and the mother
is in our postnatal unit and is fairly comfortable, considering her ordeal. Well, our five minutes is up, Dr

Morgan. Let's go and see how Mrs Bewley is progressing. . .' Her voice trailed away as she looked through the glass door and saw Mr Delaware striding past the nurses' station.

Hannah followed the thin, agile navy blue-clad figure out into the obstetrics corridor, deciding that, although Sister Gregson preached calm and unflappability, she would certainly be able to move swiftly in times of emergency.

Mrs Bewley screwed up her tired eyes as she scanned the assembled group around her bed, until they came to rest on the nice lady doctor who had made the decision to keep her in.

Hannah moved to the bedside and took hold of her patient's hand. She could see the strain showing on her face and wanted to ease the transition through the stages of this difficult labour.

'Has anybody told Dave, my husband, I'm staying in?' Mrs Bewley asked.

Hannah nodded. 'Yes, we've got a message through to his place of work. He'll be here as soon as he can make it, Mrs Bewley.'

'I wish you'd call me Pamela, because——' The patient stopped in mid-sentence and grimaced.

'Your contractions are starting, Pamela,' Hannah said gently. 'We're going to give you something to help you.'

She glanced at the consultant. Simon Delaware nodded in agreement as he drew Hannah aside.

'Minimal dose,' he urged. 'We don't want to slow the contractions. I'll set up the Entonox machine so she can get some relief from breathing into the mask. The sooner we deliver this baby the better. If the labour doesn't progress quickly enough we'll have to do a Caesar.'

Half an hour elapsed with very little progression, and then the contractions started to come thick and fast. It was all hands on deck as Pamela Bewley was wheeled into Delivery. Her startled husband, arriving in the room at the same time as the head of his infant son appeared, said he would prefer to sit outside in the obstetrics waiting-room, claiming that he didn't like hospitals. They made him nervous.

This fear of hospitals must run in the family, Hannah thought as she and Simon Delaware eased the baby's shoulders out into the birth canal. She was feeling terribly relieved that this had been a successful delivery. As she looked up at the sweaty brow of the consultant she could see that he was feeling exactly the same. It could so easily have been otherwise if the birth had been delayed.

The baby's head was an alarming shade of purple, due to his precipitate birth, but within minutes of Simon Delaware cutting the cord the tiny boy was a better colour and howling healthily.

'He's wonderful!' Pamela Bewley exclaimed as she cuddled her newborn son.

After a couple of minutes, Hannah took the precious bundle away so that she could remove the excess mucus from his tiny nostrils. Then it was time for Sister Gregson to take over.

'Four pounds nine ounces,' Sister announced as she settled the newly cleaned baby into an incubator. 'Has Master Bewley got a name, Pamela?'

Pamela Bewley smiled, running a damp hand through her tousled brown hair spread out on the pillow. 'To be honest, Sister, I've been so miserable these last few weeks, with the headache and everything, I just couldn't think. We'll ask his dad when he comes in.'

Dave Bewley announced, without hesitation, that his son was to be called William Harry, after the young princes. As he sat holding his wife's hand Hannah said, 'So you see, Mr Bewley, hospitals are really very friendly places when you get used to them. If you have another baby, maybe we shall see more of you and your wife before the actual event. We do have a very good antenatal service for our mothers.'

'Oh, we'll be having more,' the proud father said. 'No doubt about that.'

'Let me get my breath back first,' Pamela Bewley put in hurriedly, but Hannah noticed that she was smiling confidently and looked the picture of happiness.

Having settled mother and baby, Hannah went along to see the premature baby, Daniel Simpson, whom Simon Delaware had delivered at the scene of the car crash. She found Sara Clarkson, the junior registrar, finishing feeding the tiny baby through a narrow tube called a Jacques' catheter, positioned in Daniel's nose.

Hannah looked down at this small miracle who could so easily have been a road casualty statistic, and her eyes misted over. She adored babies, and constantly working with them hadn't taken away her awe and sense of wonder. Daniel's head was large in proportion to his body, as with all premature babies, and he had a small, triangular face and a worried expression, like an old man.

She glanced at the chart that Sara Clarkson was filling in.

'From the look of that blood chemistry result, I think we'd better give Daniel some glucose and bicarbonate intravenously,' Hannah said. 'That should relieve his breathing problems and prevent too much acid forming in his little body.'

Simon Delaware arrived as she was saying this and nodded in agreement. 'Don't worry, Sara,' he told his junior registrar. 'Dr Morgan and I will fix that up. Go and have a rest. You'll probably be called out later.'

Sara Clarkson flashed her boss a grateful smile. Hannah noticed the same adoring expression on her face that she'd seen with Staff Nurse Phillips. She found herself hoping that this devotion virus wasn't catching!

The intensive care sister brought along a trolley with the equipment they needed to set up the IV. Hannah couldn't help admiring the way Simon Delaware coaxed one of the tiny veins into receiving the intravenous needle.

'Poor little lamb,' he said gently. 'Here I am again, inflicting more tubes on you. But it's for your own good, young man.'

He glanced up at Hannah, who was trying to conceal a smile as she prepared a piece of plaster to hold the cannula in place on the baby's arm.

'He's a tough little guy,' Simon Delaware said. 'I didn't give much for his chances out there on the road. I had to pull his mother out of the burning car and deliver the baby on the grass verge. It seemed an awful long time before I got him to breathe. And then the ambulance arrived and I got some oxygen to him. It was touch and go, I can tell you. Well, we can leave him in the nurses' capable hands for a while. Go and get some rest.'

Hannah nodded. 'Excellent idea.'

She was definitely warming to this consultant and wondering, as Staff Nurse Phillips had, what exactly it was that made him tick. What was it about him that had everyone eating out of his hand?

CHAPTER TWO

HANNAH'S feet barely touched the ground during her first month at Moortown General. There was so much to learn, so much to do, and so many changes in medical procedure to adapt to. She'd been at St Teresa's in London far too long, she realised, and had got set in her ways. Now, in this different hospital environment, she had to be constantly on her toes.

Her new boss seemed extremely considerate on the surface, but, at the same time, he managed to get maximum work-load out of her. On her rare half-days off she drove over to Lammendale to see her parents, and found the country air on the farm invigorating. She always returned to hospital feeling that she had recharged her batteries, and was able to cope much better with her patients.

When baby Daniel Simpson was a month old, Hannah took him out of his incubator and proudly installed him in a cot in the special baby unit.

'Bring the scales, Sister,' she said as she checked her tiny patient's pulse on the anterior fontanelle of his small, fair-haired head.

'Four pounds five ounces!' Sister announced as she placed the baby back in his cot. 'You'll soon be big enough to go home, Daniel. Have you heard how his mother is, Dr Morgan? She hasn't been in to see Daniel for a couple of days.'

'Let's see. We discharged her two weeks ago, didn't

we? So she's due in Outpatients for her monthly check-up this morning—which reminds me, I'd better get a move on.'

Staff Nurse Rona Phillips was making up the examination couch when Hannah arrived at her consulting-room. It was ten minutes before her first patient was due but already the waiting-room was almost full. She turned on the computer to check on the morning's patients. Now she'd got to grips with the machine she wondered how she'd ever coped without it.

'Ah, yes, Mrs Bewley's coming in for her monthly check-up as well,' she said as her eyes scanned the screen.

'That's our patient who had pre-eclampsia, isn't it?' Rona Phillips said, coming over to watch the screen. 'It doesn't seem like four weeks since we rushed her up to Nightingale.'

'Certainly doesn't!' Hannah agreed.

Sara Clarkson poked her head round the door, running a hand through the short fair hair that had a tendency to flop over the forehead of her elfin face when she was rushing around.

'Message from the boss. He's been delayed.'

Hannah groaned. She had a distinct feeling of *déjà vu*.

'Problems with the emergency Caesarean we admitted last night. He'll be a few minutes late, so I'm to apologise to his initial patients. No need for you to take them over, Hannah.'

Hannah felt a sense of relief. A few minutes wouldn't make much difference. She smiled at Sara.

'Thanks for telling me. Have you got a long list?'

Sara nodded. 'But I've got a half-day, so I'm feeling on top of the world! See you lunchtime.'

'Fine!' In the month that she had been here, Hannah had found Sara Clarkson to be a real friend. The junior registrar had trained at Moortown General and knew everything there was to know about the place. She'd answered all Hannah's questions and filled her in on all the gossip about hospital personnel. Hannah knew she would have found it much harder to settle in without her.

Rona Phillips brought Mrs Bewley in, clutching her young son William Harry.

'Oh, isn't he gorgeous?' Rona crowed as she took the baby from his mother's arms.

Hannah smiled down at the tiny scrap. He stared back with a solemn expression in his pale blue eyes.

'He's as good as gold,' Pamela Bewley said. 'Sleeps from his ten o'clock feed until four or five in the morning.'

'He certainly seems to be thriving,' Hannah said. 'Let's unwrap him and take a closer look.'

She went through all the tests required in the monthly check-up and pronounced him to be in excellent health. Pamela Bewley was examined next, and everything appeared healthy and normal.

'I expect we'll see you next year, Mrs Bewley,' Rona quipped.

The patient laughed. 'Maybe! You will if Dave has anything to do with it. He says if they're all like William he'd like a football team.'

The door opened and Simon Delaware looked in. 'Did you get my message, Dr Morgan? Why, Mrs

Bewley, how nice to see you—and young William. My, you've grown!'

Simon Delaware spent a couple of minutes chatting to his ex-patient. Hannah had noticed that he always gave the appearance of having plenty of time, even when he was rushed off his feet. Little by little the man was getting through to her. She hated to admit it but she couldn't help admiring him. But she wasn't going to join his fan club, along with all the rest.

Valerie Simpson, mother of baby Daniel, came in halfway through the morning. Considering her ordeal on the motorway, Hannah found she was in remarkably good shape.

'How's your husband, Mrs Simpson?' Hannah asked as she tapped the results of the examination into the computer.

'Oh, Paul could be worse, Doctor,' Valerie Simpson replied, buttoning up her blouse and tucking it into her skirt. 'I'm just on my way to see him in Orthopaedics. He gets very depressed, lying there all day in that awful traction apparatus. How long before they take him off it?'

'That's up to the orthopaedic doctors. A fractured femur can take several weeks to heal.'

And often longer, Hannah thought, but she kept her opinion to herself. Life wasn't easy for Valerie at the moment. Glancing at the notes, she saw that her patient was only nineteen, her husband the same age. Hannah had heard that her husband had been breathalysed after the crash, and the results had showed him to be way over the top. It wouldn't be easy for him when he came out of hospital.

'Are you going in to see baby Daniel today?' Hannah

asked, remembering that Sister had said Valerie hadn't been in for a couple of days.

Valerie's small face puckered into a frown, and Hannah thought that this poor mother looked young enough to be still at school, and yet all the cares of the world were falling on her shoulders.

'To be honest, Doctor, I don't think I'll have time, after I've been to see Paul. Anyway, he's too young to know whether I see him or not. It won't make any difference.'

'But I thought you'd want to see him.'

There was such a thing as bonding between mother and child. It worried Hannah to see this young woman's indifference. To her dismay, she saw Valerie Simpson shrug her shoulders.

'If you think I should, otherwise. . .'

'It's up to you, Valerie,' Hannah said quickly, not wanting to seem as if she was preaching. There was no point in trying to force a mother to bond with her child, but she would have a word with Simon Delaware about it. It wasn't going to be a good start for young Daniel.

The medical staff dining-room was crowded at lunch-time. Hannah picked up her tray from the serving counter and was relieved to recognise Sara Clarkson's diminutive figure at a corner table. The junior registrar waved her hand for Hannah to join her.

'Thanks for saving me a seat,' she said as she sank down next to Sara.

'You've chosen shepherd's pie again, Hannah,' Sara said. 'Didn't you have that yesterday?'

Hannah grinned. 'Probably. It makes me feel at

home. My mother is always dishing up shepherd's pie on the farm.'

'That's a coincidence! I'm a farmer's daughter too. I was born in the Lake District. Where were you born?'

'In Wales. My parents like to consider themselves farmers now but they actually started out as teachers, who settled over here in Yorkshire and bought a small farm. It's a long story but. . .'

Her voice trailed away as she watched Simon Delaware crossing the crowded dining-room to stand in front of her.

'Are you free this evening, Hannah?' she heard him say above the hubbub of plates clattering and voices mingling with one another.

'That depends,' she said guardedly, hating the way her heart started to pound. 'Theoretically, I've got an evening off, but if Sara's off duty as well. . .'

'But have you got something planned for this evening?'

'I really must wash my hair.'

It was the first thing that came into her head and a complete fabrication. She never spent more than five minutes over her shoulder-length brown hair under the shower. A further five minutes with the hairdryer made it presentable.

He gave what she thought was a surprisingly boyish grin for a man who was probably approaching forty.

'Your hair looks lovely as it is. It can wait another day. I'd like to take you out for a meal so we can discuss how you're finding the work and settling in. Eight o'clock OK?'

She found herself nodding her assent. The moment

he'd left the table she turned to look at Sara, who seemed to be holding herself in check.

'Don't look so worried,' Sara said. 'I could have told you this would happen. He took me out after a month. I think he has to make some kind of written assessment to the Board of Governors.'

'Well, that's all right, then. For a moment I thought he fancied me!'

Sara burst out laughing. 'You must be joking. Simon Delaware doesn't fancy anybody. He's a love-'em-and-leave-'em man. Loads of one-night stands but never takes anyone out twice.'

'You're exaggerating!'

'No, I'm not. He takes everybody out once and that's it. They never get another bite at the cherry. But we all live in hope. I suppose that's one of the reasons we're always so helpful. But I don't know anyone who's had more than one date with him.'

Hannah pushed her plate to one side. Despite her initial decision to keep Simon Delaware at arm's length, she couldn't help admitting that he fascinated her. She'd never met anyone like him. And the idea that no one had succeeded in going on a second date intrigued her.

'I bet I could get a second date with him,' she heard herself saying.

Sara grinned. 'Bet you couldn't. I've told you. He's taking you out to give you a month's assessment and that will be that.'

'You really think so? I'm sure if I turned on the charm, like the rest of you do, he'd succumb and ask me out again. I'm the only female in this hospital who doesn't go around smarming up to him. If I suddenly changed my tune, he'd be so flabbergasted he'd definitely want to see me again.'

'Bet you twenty pounds you can't get a second date!'

'You're on!' Hannah said. 'We'll make it a bet to our favourite charities. Mine's Save the Children.'

'Well, that's a pity, 'cos they won't get a penny,' Sara said with a wry grin. 'You're on to a loser, I'm afraid.'

'Don't be too sure,' Hannah said, with a confidence that was rapidly evaporating.

Nightingale Wing was quiet when Hannah went off duty, leaving the two housemen, dark-haired James Dewhirst and fair-haired David Ratcliffe, in charge of the Delaware firm. She felt confident in their capabilities. Dr Dewhirst in particular was proving to be an excellent doctor. Although only recently qualified, he was thirty years old, having had a career in marketing before going to medical school, so his relative maturity meant that he was always someone Hannah could rely on.

She'd had a brief note from the boss during the afternoon, saying that he would pick her up outside the residents' quarters at eight. He had arranged for the housemen to be on duty while they were away and he didn't predict any problems.

It was a beautiful summer evening as they drove out through the car park and headed for the hills beyond Moortown. The road climbed higher and higher away from the sprawling urbanisation, until they reached the top of one of Hannah's favourite hills, where a view of the Yorkshire Dales spread out before them.

Simon stopped the car in front of the Coach and

Horses and Hannah got out and looked at the wild countryside around her. The pub was set back from the winding country lane. Although they were only a few miles outside Moortown, it seemed like a different world.

Hannah stretched her long legs as she got out of Simon Delaware's silver two-seater sports car, thinking how typical it was that he should have a flashy, expensive car like this! She was wearing brand new, cream leather shoes, with higher than usual heels, to give her confidence in her dealings with this tall, charismatic consultant.

A warm summer breeze blew her brown shoulder-length hair across her face. She draped her white woollen sweater across her shoulders, partially covering her summer-tanned bare arms. It was still warm, but the short-sleeved cream linen dress was very light-weight. She *felt* confident. . .so far!

She'd noticed Simon Delaware's eyes momentarily straying from the road once or twice as he seemed to check out her appearance. She'd applied just enough Coco Chanel to tease his nostrils without overpowering him. Maybe she was overdressed for a country pub, but she had a job to do. It was going to be such fun if she managed to get that second date!

She took a deep breath of the fresh moorland air as she considered her strategy. She wanted him to notice her as a woman, as well as a colleague. She was more likely to get that second date fixed if he was attracted to her.

'Mmm, I love it up here!' she exclaimed, flicking her dark hair behind her ears.

She looked around and saw that Simon Delaware

was smiling in amusement as he locked the car. Had she said something funny?

'So why did you spend so long in London?' he asked, coming round the car to stand beside her as she took in the breathtaking view of the moors, stretching as far as the eye could see and smouldering mysteriously under the last rays of the summer sun.

'I thought it would be a good idea to move away for my medical training; everyone always told me to spend some time in London while I was still young. I enjoyed it, but it's a relief to be home again.'

'Where's home exactly?' he asked as they started to walk slowly across the cobbled yard to the pub entrance.

'About ten miles in that direction.' Hannah shielded her eyes as she pointed westward. The sun was dipping low on the horizon and its fierce rays were very strong to the naked eye. 'My parents live near a little village called Greystones in Lammendale. Where do you live, Mr Delaware?'

She slipped the question in as casually as she could. He needn't think this getting to know each other was going to be all one-sided!

'Call me Simon,' he said, opening the pub door and ushering her in, but ignoring her question.

The bar was small and cosy, and in spite of the warm summer evening a fire had been lit in the wide stone grate. It glowed in the background, giving a homely atmosphere to the stark, uneven stone-flagged floor, the timbered walls and low ceilings. They chose a round, roughly carved wooden table by a window that looked out across the moors to the distant fells.

Hannah watched as Simon Delaware brought the

drinks over from the bar. He looked relaxed, informal, at ease—not a bit like a consultant, apart from the tall, impressive stance. He'd chatted amiably to the barman with the same casual manner he used with his patients.

She made a mental note to remember to keep turning on the charm, intent on winning her bet but thinking also that it would be no hardship having a second date. He was an interesting man, not to mention being good-looking in a rugged sort of way. Easy on the eye, enjoyable to be with. . .

She leaned back against the wooden seat. Yes, she'd enjoyed zooming along the dual carriageway in his super car and then noting the ease with which he negotiated the narrow lanes, chatting all the while about inconsequential things—books, theatre, cinema. Oh, yes, they had a lot in common and a second date would be fun, especially knowing that she'd won the bet.

But, meanwhile, she would enjoy the first one and not count her chickens until they were hatched. She picked up her glass of wine. Simon, she noticed, was drinking Perrier. That was reassuring in view of the tortuous drive home.

He asked her how she found the work at Moortown. She replied that it was interesting. Were there any problems with the staff? She said everyone had been most helpful. They went on to discuss a couple of complicated obstetric cases and Hannah felt he was testing her at this stage. But, after a few minutes, he seemed satisfied, and she could tell that the professional side of the evening was concluded. She watched him as he leaned back against his seat and visibly relaxed as he sipped his Perrier.

'I see you don't drink and drive,' she observed.

'Absolutely not!' he replied vehemently. 'I've seen too many cases of drink-driving end in tragedy. That accident last month need never have happened. Paul Simpson, the father of the baby I delivered at the roadside, had been drinking. He'd taken his pregnant wife out for a pub lunch and drunk at least five pints. He'll have to face the music when he gets out of hospital. But let's not talk shop any more. You were telling me about your family over in Lammendale. Is that where you were born?'

'No, I was born in Wales. My parents are both teachers and they moved to Lammendale to teach in the Greystones village school when I was eight. At first we had a tiny cottage in the village, but when I was twelve we bought a small farm at the top of the dale. It was going cheap because it was practically derelict. My parents spent all their spare time rebuilding and renovating it. We all loved that place. . .still do. My parents are so happy in their retirement there. Where do you come from, Simon?'

She held her breath, hoping she hadn't broken the rapport that was striking up between them.

He put down his glass and gave her an enigmatic smile. 'Everywhere. . .everywhere and nowhere,' he said in a deep, husky tone. 'This is my home. . .for the moment. I live in the hospital, work in the hospital. That's my home and has been for the past year.'

His voice held a timbre of finality, a touch-me-not quality. She longed to probe him further but she was afraid to break up the amicable feeling running between them. Besides, she had a mission to fulfil! He was unlikely to ask for a second date with someone who posed too many personal questions.

'And do you have brothers and sisters?' he was asking her now. Really, this was all so one-sided! But she didn't dare turn the tables.

She shook her head. 'I'm an only one.' She longed to say, how about you? But she held back her curiosity.

They scanned the bar menu together and chose the dish of the day, which turned out to be a delicious oxtail casserole with dumplings and mashed potatoes. Hannah realised how hungry she'd been as she finished the last mouthful and sat back in her seat to look out across the darkened moorland. Lights twinkled from a small hamlet lower down the valley. She felt replete and very content, and totally at ease as she declined a second glass of wine. She must keep her wits about her, both for the boss and in case she was called on to the wards during the night.

'Do you think you're going to enjoy working at Moortown General?' Simon Delaware asked.

She looked across the table at this man from nowhere and recognised the characteristics that Sara Clarkson had pointed out. He seemed interested in her—perhaps a shade too interested in her background, but then this was supposed to be a getting-to-know-you exercise. She was glad she'd nothing to hide!

But he didn't seem approachable. Oh, he was fine with the patients. She'd noticed on that very first day in hospital how kind and gentle he was; he'd shown such a lovely, soothing manner with Pamela Bewley, their pre-eclampsia patient, coaxing her along every step of the way and giving her confidence. The warmth had been there during that difficult birth and all the others when they'd worked alongside since then. But now, although they'd been together for nearly two hours, she hadn't broken through his outer shell.

'You haven't answered my question,' he said, leaning towards her across the table.

She realised that she'd been staring at him, weighing up what made him tick. She smiled her most charming smile, feeling guilty at her subterfuge.

'I'm going to love working at Moortown General,' she said, with an enthusiasm that was only slightly more than genuine.

'Good.' He was smiling back now, but only with his mouth. The dark eyes remained impassive. 'Talking of which, I think we should be getting back.'

He was holding open the outer door for Hannah when her heart missed a beat. Outside in the car park, right beside the door, her parents were climbing out of their distinctive Land Rover and chattering amiably as they approached the pub.

Her mother stopped dead in her tracks. 'Hannah, what a lovely surprise! We only popped out for a quick drink. Well, it was such a lovely evening. Now, come on, introduce me to your friend.'

'This is Simon Delaware—my parents, Gwen and Gareth Morgan.'

'Delighted to meet you, Mrs Morgan, Mr Morgan.'

Hannah held back as her boss shook hands. Her mother, she noticed, was beaming all over her face, and kept looking towards Hannah, mouthing something incomprehensible.

It became immediately apparent what Gwen Morgan was trying to ask Hannah as she said to Simon, 'We live in the next valley from here. We've got a farm in

Lammendale. You must get Hannah to bring you over to see us one day soon. Pop across one afternoon. You'd be most welcome.'

'We're rarely off duty together, Mum,' Hannah put in hurriedly.

And then, suddenly, a wicked thought crossed her mind. Why not? Why not persuade Simon to go over to Lammendale with her. Wouldn't that constitute a second date? She might yet win her bet with Sara!

'Although I suppose we might be able to arrange something,' she heard herself saying. Her eyes met Simon's and she saw his startled expression.

'Oh, do try and come!' Hannah's mother was saying as she looked up at Simon.

Hannah saw he was hesitating. He won't come, she thought. He's simply being polite. Not jumping in too soon to show that the whole idea is preposterous. He'll make some excuse that. . .

'I think I could possibly arrange it one day soon. . . perhaps next Wednesday,' Hannah was amazed to hear him say.

'Wednesday would be fine!' Gwen Morgan said. 'Well, goodbye you two.'

'Goodbye,' Hannah said, feeling a mixture of embarassment and triumph. She'd secured that second date! Sara would be amazed!

As they drove back towards Moortown Hannah kept the inconsequential conversation flowing, hoping that Simon wasn't having second thoughts about going to see the farm.

He parked in his reserved space in the staff car park. She climbed out, and together they walked the last few steps towards the residents' quarters. Inside the lobby, at the foot of the impressive stone staircase leading up into the hospital, dominated by a carved stone bust of Alexander Fleming, he turned to go along the corridor leading to the hallowed rooms reserved for consultants and visiting dignitaries. Her room was in the other direction.

'I've enjoyed the evening,' she began, hating herself for her duplicity. If she hadn't been doing this for a bet would she have turned on the charm quite so much?

He looked down at her, his expression pleasant but distant. 'So have I.'

'What I mean is, I'm glad you're going to come over to see our farm,' she improvised desperately, her words tumbling out in a breathless torrent. 'It's so beautiful over there in the summer—unlike the winter, when we get snowed up for weeks on end and. . .'

'Yes, I'd like to see it.'

She swallowed as she looked up into the deep brown eyes. They were giving nothing away, as dark, mysterious and enigmatic as ever. But she'd clinched that second date! She almost whooped for joy! Well, at least the date had been suggested and he'd acquiesced, said the small voice of conscience. Was that the same thing? But he could have said no, or at the very least. . .

'Dr Morgan!' The hall porter was hurrying towards them. 'And Mr Delaware, too. I've been trying to contact both of you. Dr Dewhirst needs some help with one of your patients on Nightingale.'

Simon Delaware was already striding over to the hall porter's phone.

'Breathing problems with the prem we delivered by

Caesarean section last night,' he reported back tersely. 'Come on.'

James Dewhirst was relieved to see them when they arrived at the special care unit.

'I was worried about Peter's colour,' he said. 'He was becoming cyanosed and turning blue. I had to disconnect him from the ventilator for a brief period for intensive suction; when I reconnected his colour improved.'

'Good.' The consultant reached inside the incubator to examine the frail little infant. 'One of us should be with him for the next few hours. His lungs are dangerously immature. I'll take the first turn while it's critical. You'd better get some sleep, James. You can work the morning shift. Hannah, will you come back in about four hours and stay for a couple of hours? I'll come back and relieve you in the early hours, by which time I would hope we could make a better prognosis.'

As Hannah walked back down the corridor towards her room she saw Sara standing outside her room fiddling with her key. The junior registrar's face lit up when she saw Hannah approaching.

'Well, how was it?'

Hannah's concern for baby Peter had pushed all thoughts of the evening's outing from her mind. It now seemed so inconsequential when viewed in the light of her professional work here. She felt almost ashamed of behaving like a carefree teenager earlier on, but she reminded herself that she couldn't let her professional problems take over her whole life. She had to let her hair down occasionally.

She smiled. 'A piece of cake, really. He couldn't wait to say let's meet again soon.'

'You're joking!'

'No, I'm not. We're going out next Wednesday afternoon. We've both got a half-day.'

She stopped in the middle of the corridor as she
broke the news to her colleague. The vague feelings
of guilt still hovered as she saw the amazed expression
on Sara's face.

'Look. . .I have to admit, I did engineer things a
bit,' she explained quickly. 'I mean. . .'

'Meaning what, exactly?'

Sara's mouth was set in a straight line but Hannah
was relieved to see that her eyes were dancing with
humour. Oh good, she wasn't taking this silly bet any
more seriously than she was. It was just light-hearted
fun between friends; a bit of a giggle.

'Well, actually, we bumped into my mum and dad
outside the pub and they invited him to come out to
see their farm. So, technically speaking, he didn't ask
me for a second date. We asked him. So I don't know
where we stand as far as the bet is concerned. I certainly couldn't let you cough up twenty pounds, even
if it is for charity.'

'Well, thanks for being so honest,' Sara said, running
a hand through her short blonde hair as she eyed
Hannah shrewdly. 'But I've got to admit you've
astounded me. Even allowing for the fact that you
suggested the second date, I'm amazed that Mr
Delaware accepted. And especially taking him home
to see your mum and dad. That sort of thing doesn't
usually happen until a couple are practically engaged
to be married!'

'Oh, don't be so archaic!'

'Your mum mightn't be thinking so! Taking home

a good catch like a consultant obstetrician. If she's anything like mine, your mum will hear wedding-bells.'

'My mum's not like that. I'm thirty years old and a confirmed bachelor-girl—unless somebody comes along to bowl me over, which isn't likely in this neck of the woods.'

'Not even Simon Delaware?'

'Especially not Simon Delaware!' Hannah answered emphatically, realising suddenly that she was desperately trying to convince herself. It had been a few years since she'd had any sort of meaningful relationship. She'd gone out with a few of the doctors at St Teresa's over the years she'd been there. One in particular had roused her interest, and they'd had a passionate relationship for a few months, but she hadn't wanted to get too involved at that stage of her career so she'd deliberately cooled it. He'd got married to a theatre sister, she remembered. Then there had been the senior registrar who'd offloaded his work on to her while she was his junior. She'd gone out with him and allowed herself to be wined and dined, but when he'd wanted her to go to bed with him she'd drawn the line and stopped doing his extra work at the same time.

'Well, I think you deserve an A for effort, even if you did bend the rules, Hannah. I'm a woman of my word, so I insist on paying something.'

'Why don't we call it a draw? Ten pounds each?'

'Agreed!' Sara smiled. 'It was my idea, so I've got to cough up after all your machinations. Besides, you've still got to get through the meet-the-family ordeal. It will be worth ten pounds to hear all about that! Come back for coffee and we'll write out our cheques. Mine will go to the local hospice. Which charity did you say for yours?'

'Save the Children,' Hannah replied, glad that some good was coming out of her complicated social life.

It took Hannah a while to get to sleep after her coffee with Sara. She'd drunk weak, instant decaffeinated, so it wasn't the caffeine that was keeping her awake. She was dead tired, and only had about three hours left in which to recuperate, but the events of the previous day were jumping around in her head.

Eventually they all got jumbled up together into a vivid dream, where she was trying to resuscitate the little prem, Peter, in her mother's kitchen while Simon Delaware was looking on and criticising her every move.

She awoke with a start and put out her hand to silence the alarm clock. Three-thirty in the morning. She was definitely not feeling her best! Dragging a white coat over cotton trousers and shirt, she padded out into the deserted corridor.

'Keep a clear airway,' Simon Delaware instructed as she took over. 'The mucus keeps building up, so you need to monitor the suction apparatus constantly. But for such a tiny chap he's got a good fighting spirit.'

He put his hand in the incubator and gave the tiny figure a playful stroke on the cheek before looking back at Hannah.

'Did you sleep?'

'Sort of,' she replied.

The bland expression in his eyes changed. For an instant she thought he looked concerned. . .yes, there was real concern there, as if he really cared about the welfare of his staff as much as his patients.

'I'll be back in a couple of hours,' he said. 'You can have some time off during the day. I don't want you to start falling down on the job.'

The enigmatic smile on his lips, coupled with the caring expression in his eyes, gave her an inner emotional jolt. For the first time she reviewed him as a man, rather than a pawn in a silly game, and came to the conclusion that she'd misjudged him. The warmth was there. . .but how to find it was the question. And why should she care anyway? Save the Children were ten pounds better off, and when she'd discharged her social obligations next Wednesday that would be the end of it.

But would it?

As she watched him walking away through the swing doors she found herself wondering if she'd bitten off more than she could chew. Because this whole incident was disturbing her more than she cared to admit.

She leaned over the incubator and gave baby Peter all her attention.

CHAPTER THREE

WEDNESDAY afternoon. The sun's rays reflected in the polished silver sheen of Simon Delaware's car as the streets of Moortown were left behind in the valley and they reached the open road ahead.

Hannah knew she should have been feeling happy at the prospect of her half-day, but she couldn't get rid of the butterflies in her stomach. Glancing sideways at the man beside her, she felt even more apprehensive.

It had been just as Sara Clarkson had predicted when Hannah had phoned her mother.

'I'm so glad you're bringing your consultant over to see the farm. How long have you known him? What did he say his name was? Simon Delaware? That's a nice name; good, solid. . .'

'Mum, we're only going to drop in for a few minutes and. . .'

'Nonsense! I'm going to make you a proper tea. I'll bake some of those nice scones you like, and a Victoria sponge. How old is this Simon? He didn't look very old, but then. . .'

Reviewing the embarassing phone conversation as the car sped along the road towards Lammendale, Hannah groaned inwardly as she realised what she'd let herself in for.

'What did you say, Hannah?' Simon Delaware asked, his eyes momentarily glancing her way.

'I didn't say anything,' she replied quickly. 'I was simply admiring the view. Even though I've spent years here I never get bored with it.'

'You're a real country-lover, aren't you? So am I.'

'Really? I would have taken you for a townie.'

'I've lived in both town and country, but I prefer the country.'

Hannah relaxed against the soft leather of her seat and smiled to herself. He was opening up. Perhaps it was a good idea coming out to see Mum and Dad, after all. Her mother would certainly find out more than she could about this mysterious man.

'It's Simon, isn't it?' Gwen Morgan said, beaming happily as they went in through the kitchen door. She patted the back of her neat grey hair and positioned her spectacles in a manner which Hannah had seen her use with her young pupils at the Greystones Primary School, recognising it was a sign that she meant business. Her mother was going to impart information, but she was also going to find out everything she could about a particular subject. On this occasion the subject was Simon.

'Hannah has told me so much about you, haven't you, Hannah? We'll have a cup of tea so we can all get to know each other before we show you round the farm.'

Cups of tea at the kitchen table broke the ice and Hannah marvelled at the way Simon fielded the barrage of questions. But then she reminded herself that he'd had a lot of practice. It amused her to think that if he'd been one of her mother's pupils he would definitely have been detained in the classroom at playtime for failing to give adequate answers!

Her father came in from the fields and started eulogising about the joys of retirement on the farm. Hannah had always noticed that when he spoke on any subject concerning life in the country his whole face lit up; his weatherbeaten cheeks had the appearance of having been shone with furniture polish until they resembled the rosy apples that he'd managed to persuade the gnarled old trees in his minuscule orchard to produce—in spite of the fact that the local born-and-bred Yorkshiremen had told him it couldn't be done. She remembered that there had been a certain amount of resentment when this teacher from the Welsh valleys had started farming on the hitherto barren hillside, but, nearly twenty years on, Gareth Morgan was now well and truly accepted, admired and respected for his success with the farm and his good works in the rural community as a parish councillor.

'I'll get tea ready while Dad shows you round the farm,' Mrs Morgan said.

'I thought we'd just had tea,' Simon Delaware said as they walked across the cobbled farmyard.

Hannah smiled. 'That was just something to push us along until proper teatime. In Yorkshire, the kettle is continually on the boil.'

The grand tour of the eighteenth-century farm then took place: Simon Delaware was shown round the barn, the mistle with its six cows, the milking-machines, and the large enclosure where fifty hens wandered around contentedly outside their henhouse, while Gareth Morgan explained that he didn't agree with battery farming.

'I don't make a profit on this place, Mr Delaware,' he said, in a tone that hinted he was proud of the fact. 'It's my hobby. Always has been, even when I was teaching all day and marking books in the evening. I simply love the life we have here.'

They walked part of the way up the hillside to see some of the fifty sheep that roamed the fells above them, each sheep proudly bearing the M for Morgan stamp on its back.

'Reared for their wool,' Hannah explained to Simon. 'Dad would never bring himself to have them killed for meat.'

Gwen Morgan came out into the farmyard to meet them on their return. Rubbing her hands dry on a teatowel, she was looking happy at the prospect of teatime with this charming young friend of her daughter's.

Hannah noticed that she'd removed the capacious flowered overall she always wore in the kitchen to reveal, as she had expected, that she was wearing one of her 'Sunday best' dresses. A brown linen neatly tailored frock, which was always worn with an antique silver and emerald brooch pinned at the neckline.

'Let's not stand around out here; I expect Simon is wanting a cup of tea, and I've been baking, so I hope you're all hungry.'

As Hannah worked her way through home-cooked ham with salad, home-baked bread, scones and cakes, she noticed that the walk up the fells had sharpened Simon's appetite too.

'If we were in hospital, we would be working through the afternoon with no prospect of food until the evening, but here we are, enjoying ourselves as if we'd been digging ditches,' Simon remarked.

Gwen Morgan beamed at her guest, and Hannah thought that was exactly the sort of remark to endear Simon to her mother. She hoped she wasn't getting the wrong idea about this visit and reading too much into it.

'You will come again, won't you, Simon, now that you know where we live?' was the parting shot from Gwen Morgan as they drove away through the farm gates.

She was definitely getting the wrong idea! Hannah thought. She noticed that Simon merely smiled, but they were too far away for him to reply. He'd been profuse in his thanks for the splendid teatime spread, but reticent in every other area of chat and questioning.

'I hope you didn't find all this Welsh/Yorkshire family welcome too overwhelming,' Hannah said as Simon negotiated the winding bends leading down to the river that wound through Lammendale.

'I thought it was charming,' he replied, unexpectedly pulling the car into the side of the road and switching off the engine. He turned towards her, a quiet smile on his lips. 'Now, tell me what you're really up to.'

She was taken completely off-guard. 'I don't know what you mean.'

He laughed. 'Oh, yes, you do. You're up to something. I've seen you and Sara Clarkson getting your heads together. I'm truly grateful for the hospitality your parents showed me, I wouldn't have missed it for anything, but all this pseudo-charm you've been lavishing upon me has been so uncharacteristic of you, Hannah. When we met up with your parents so unexpectedly last week, I saw your initial reaction to your mother's invitation. And then, seconds later, you seemed to turn it to your advantage. Again, it was so out of character that I decided I had to take you up on it. Come on, come clean! What's going on?'

She drew in her breath as she leaned back against the seat. The hot sun was dazzling her through the windscreen and she put a hand over her eyes. Better admit the game was up.

'Was it so obvious?' she asked in a small voice.

He smiled. 'You were totally transparent—to me at any rate. I can tell when someone is putting on an act. What's it all about?'

She swallowed. 'Sara and I had a bet on with each other. She bet me that I couldn't get a second date with you. She said you only ever took girls out once.'

'Well, well, that is interesting!' The smile broadened. 'And you don't mind?'

'Mind? Why should I mind? I hadn't realised they'd all noticed about my one-date rule.'

'So it's a fact? You make a point of having only one date with people? But why on earth would you do that?'

'Maybe I don't want to get involved,' he said slowly.

'But why? You're not. . . Are you married?'

His eyes held a veiled expression as he replied, 'No. . .no, I'm not married.'

'Then. . .'

'Let's leave it at that, shall we? No more questions. I can't stand the way everyone tries to interrogate me.'

And then, to her amazement, he leaned across and lightly brushed her lips with his own.

As he pulled away she could feel her heart fluttering.

In spite of her determination not to join the fan club, she would have to be made of stone not to succumb to his charms.

'Time to move on,' he said under his breath, almost to himself.

But Hannah heard and understood. He was probably already regretting the fact that he'd let down his guard. Especially with a colleague, someone he would have to work with every day.

The evening round on Nightingale Wing took longer than usual. Simon kept breaking off to deal with individual patients at great length. Hannah could see that the group of medical students who'd joined the registrars, housemen and consultant were sureptitiously glancing at their watches with a view to excusing themselves as soon as was feasibly possible.

They finished up with a full examination of baby Peter. Now five days old, he was still in his incubator for most of the day, but had been taken off the ventilator.

'He's not yet out of the woods, but I'm more confident every day that he'll pull through,' Simon said. 'So that concludes the round this evening. Any more questions, ladies and gentlemen?'

The medical students were free to go. The two housemen went down to the delivery room to prepare for a Caesarean that Simon was going to perform later that evening and Sara Clarkson and Hannah helped Sister to settle the mothers in the postnatal ward, after which they joined her in her office for coffee. Simon declined, saying that he wanted to check what was happening in Theatre.

When Sister Gregson went off to give her day report to the newly arrived night nurses at the nurses' station, Sara tackled Hannah about the afternoon on the farm.

'Was it an ordeal? I know you were dreading it.'

'Actually, I enjoyed it. Simon is. . . Well, I hate to admit it, but he's really good to be with.'

'Good to be with! The understatement of the year! What you mean is, you're falling under the spell, like the rest of us.'

'I'm not sure.' Hannah hesitated. 'I don't think there'd be any point because. . .'

The door opened and Simon walked in.

'I'd like you to help me with the Caesarean in half an hour; Theatre Two,' he said, his mouth curving into an amused smile as he looked at the two of them. 'What are you hatching now? No, don't tell me. I don't wish to know.'

He was out of the door before either of them could reply.

'What did he mean by that?' Sara asked.

'I had to tell him. . .about the bet. He. . .'

'You told him about the bet! But why?'

'He'd rumbled me. Said he knew I was putting on an act, so. . .'

'So you confessed. And was he annoyed?'

'No, he seemed to find it amusing.'

'Well, that's a relief. What did you find out about him?'

'Nothing. Absolutely nothing.'

Hannah wasn't going to commit herself, wasn't going to admit that he'd said he wasn't married, because the hesitant manner he'd adopted when he said that had belied the words. She was convinced he was involved in some sort of important relationship. Otherwise why would he have this self-imposed one-date rule?

Theatre Two was ablaze with lights. Hannah felt her strength and confidence returning as she pushed aside her personal problems and gave all her attention to the patient. Simon, at the other side of the table, had barely looked at her when they scrubbed up together but now, as he was about to make the first incision, he looked across the table.

'This patient will be new to you, Dr Morgan, so let me fill you in on the case-history. This is Madeleine Carter, age thirty-two, first pregnancy. She has placenta praevia.'

He glanced across to the back of the theatre to the four medical students, who were scribbling furiously in their notebooks. 'And placenta praevia is what kind of condition?'

One of the students, an intense, likeable, fair-haired young man whom Hannah had seen on the ward-round earlier that evening, spoke up.

'If the placenta, which is the pipe-line through which the baby gets its nourishment from the mother, lies wholly or partially in the lower part of the womb, it's inevitable that as the lower part stretches during the latter weeks of pregnancy there will be some separation of the placenta, causing it to bleed.'

'Exactly,' Simon said, nodding over to Hannah to pass him a scalpel. 'And in this case, at thirty-eight weeks, as there is no improvement in the condition, I've decided that Caesarean section is necessary. As most of you know, I perform Caesarean sections

only when strictly necessary. If there's any chance
of a normal delivery, that's the course of action I
prefer.'

'Why did you choose a general anaesthetic as
opposed to an epidural—the spinal anaesthetic that
blocks off the pain but leaves the patient conscious?'
Hannah asked as Simon cut through the abdominal
wall. She'd added her explanation of epidural in case
any of the students hadn't come across that method of
anaesthetic before.

'Madeleine requested it,' he replied evenly. 'She said
the less she knew about the procedure the better. But
I've promised to wake her up when the baby
arrives. . . and here she is, a dear little girl. Dr
Morgan, would you take charge of her while I suture
the wound?'

Hannah always found Caesarean sections remark-
able. To extricate a perfectly formed new baby from
the folds of the abdomen had seemed nothing short of
miraculous when she'd first seen it. And even now,
ten years on from that teaching session in Theatre
when she was a raw medical student, the excitement
and wonder were still there.

When she'd checked out the baby's lungs she handed
her to Sister for weighing.

'Seven pounds,' Sister announced, with the customary pride she always showed with all her babies.

Hannah went to strip off her theatre greens and pull
on her clothes. She would shower when she got back
to her room. It had been a long day; the morning
uneventful but strenuous on Nightingale, the afternoon
decidedly unusual out at the farm.

As she went down the steps towards the residents' quarters she held her breath. Simon was ahead of her. He turned and stood at the meeting of the corridors so that she couldn't pass without saying something.

'I'm going to make some coffee. Care to join me?' he said casually.

Her heart gave a little hop, skip and a jump. She wished she could say no, but the overwhelming desire to spend some more time with him was too much for her.

'Wouldn't that constitute a third date?' she quipped lightly.

He gave her a wry grin. 'It might, but who's counting?'

'Love some,' she heard herself saying.

She noticed that the corridor leading to Simon's room had actual carpet on it. Even the doors looked more imposing than her humble abode.

'Polished brass doorknob. Oh, very posh!' she said as he let her into his room.

He laughed. 'I must admit there are perks to being a consultant. But don't forget it's not long since I was in the ranks, so I really appreciate it. How do you take your coffee?'

'Black.' She sank down on the squashy, cretonne-covered sofa and looked around her at the large, high-ceilinged sitting-room. She could hear Simon grinding the coffee beans in the kitchen. Proper coffee! What a treat!

The phone on the coffee-table started to ring.

'Simon!' she called.

He couldn't hear above the din of the coffee-grinder. She'd better answer it. 'Hello?'

There was a short pause and then a small, childish voice said, 'I want to speak to my daddy.'

Hannah swallowed. It could be a wrong number. . . On the other hand. . .

'Who's calling?' she asked gently.

'Michael.'

'Wait a moment, Michael.'

She put the phone carefully on its side and went into the kitchen. The grinding had stopped. Simon had heard her last sentence on the phone.

'Michael wants to speak to his daddy,' she said quietly.

'Thank you.'

He was striding over to the phone.

'Michael, are you OK? What was that? So where's Adele? You're not alone, are you? That's good! Do you like your babysitter? Oh, she's waiting to put you to bed, is she? I miss you too, Michael. I'll call you again soon. Night-night, darling. Sleep well. . .'

Hannah stood in the kitchen doorway, watching Simon as he slowly put the phone down. She saw the dejected stance, the air of sadness, so uncharacteristic of this strong, confident man. But when he turned around he was his normal self again, the air of bravado firmly fixed in place.

She went towards him, wanting to say that he needn't pretend any more. Whatever relationship he was hiding was safe with her. She realised that, for some ill-defined reason, she suddenly resented the thought of his having an important relationship, but if it was there then wishing wouldn't make it go away. And why did she resent it anyway? He'd said he wasn't married. So who was Adele?

'So you're Michael's daddy,' she said gently.

'Yes. . .but I'd appreciate it if you kept that to yourself.'

'Of course I will; that goes without saying. . .but I wish you'd explain the situation.'

He turned away. 'You wouldn't understand.'

'I might. Why not try me?'

'I can't tell you any more.' His voice was poignantly husky.

'Adele wouldn't like it, would she?' Hannah said in a deadpan voice, annoyed by the sudden plummeting of her spirits. This relationship with her boss that had started out as a huge joke was becoming too involved. She didn't like the churning of her emotions, the feeling of being desperately involved. . .of caring too much. . .

'No, she wouldn't,' he said quietly.

'Who is she?'

'I can't answer that.' He moved closer and put his hands on her shoulders. 'The reason I keep myself to myself is because there are some things in my background that have to remain secret. Oh, don't get me wrong.' He gave a harsh laugh. 'Nothing criminal, but I've given my solemn promise to the people involved that my secret. . .their secret will remain just that.'

He bent forward and kissed her gently on the lips.

She felt an unwelcome rush of excitement. She didn't want to get involved with this enigmatic man, but it was already too late to hold back.

He pulled away and looked down at her with a tender expression in his dark brown eyes. 'I've told you too much.'

'You've told me nothing,' she said. 'But. . .'

'But don't ask me any more,' he cut in, his tone desperately appealing as his lips came down on hers.

She leaned against him, savouring the ripple of sensation as his sensual lips merged with hers. She was unprepared for the flaring of her own emotions. This was more than just a kiss. . .it was a deep longing, a fusing of kindred spirits. . .

He was pulling away; his eyes held a haggard, anxious look as he stared down at her, his hands gripping her shoulders.

'I shouldn't have done that. . .but sometimes I. . .'

He turned away and she heard the catch in his throat.

'Why shouldn't you have done that?' she asked softly. 'Why are you scared of becoming involved?'

He turned round slowly, his eyes full of a troubled haunting expression.

'I'm not free; I can't tell you why. But sometimes I get tired of play-acting, pretending to be someone I'm not. . .pretending to be the carefree, extrovert charmer that everyone thinks I am, when deep down. . .'

He pulled her into his arms, stroking the back of her head. 'I can't tell you more. I've given my word. And please don't repeat anything I've said tonight. My past has to remain a secret. . .as long as. . .for a long time to come.' He pulled himself away and the bright smile reappeared. 'About that coffee; come with me into the kitchen, Hannah. Help me salvage the dregs. I expect it's boiled away to nothing.'

Hannah revelled in the feeling of rapport as they sat at the kitchen table drinking coffee; they had been unbelievably close but the barrier was back again, the

touch-me-not, don't-ask-any-more-questions-because-
I've-said-too-much-already barrier.

The charming little boy on the phone had captivated
her with his endearingly childish voice. She
remembered now that he had had an American accent.
She glanced up at the kitchen clock. It was after mid-
night. Of course! Initially she'd wondered why Michael
was being put to bed so late, but if he was in the States
it would be earlier in the evening.

But who was Adele? Was she the person who'd
extracted a promise from Simon to keep an impossible
secret?

CHAPTER FOUR

JUNE had turned the corner into July; a heatwave had arrived and Hannah found herself getting very tired on the wards. Even with the windows wide open the atmosphere was hot and stuffy and made working very difficult.

'Feeling the heat, aren't you, Dr Morgan?' Sister Gregson said, putting out her hand to hold on to Hannah's arm when she'd finished writing up the treatment charts on Nightingale.

Hannah glanced up at the kindly sister and then at the ward clock. Only eleven o'clock in the morning and she was feeling exhausted. There had been an emergency Caesarean during the night and she'd had very little sleep.

She leaned against the nurses' station as she gave a wry grin to the sister she'd come to admire for her professional expertise and sympathetic attitude during the two months she'd worked at the Moortown General.

'The trouble is we're just not used to coping with extremes of heat in this country. We don't get much hot weather and when we do, if we have to work, we just grin and bear it.'

'I've ordered some cool air fans for the ward,' Sister said. 'Strategically placed, they should ease the situation. Now, are you getting enough sleep, Doctor? Were you assisting at the emergency Caesar last night?'

'She certainly was,' put in a bright and cheery masculine voice.

Hannah looked up as Simon arrived at the nurses' station, marvelling at the way he always managed to look as if he'd had a full night's sleep and hadn't a care in the world.

'Dr Morgan worked alongside me until four this morning and then we spent another hour settling in our new prem, Sister,' Simon said, his deep brown eyes warm as he glanced down at Hannah.

She felt the colour rising to her cheeks as their eyes met. She found being close to him, even in a work situation, was all too disturbing. It was so hard to handle, in view of the fact that she was no nearer finding out about the secret in Simon's past. She longed to forget all about it, but she was too heavily involved. Much to her annoyance, her emotions churned every time he came near her.

She'd discovered, in the last four weeks since that fateful night when she'd answered the phone and spoken to Simon's son, that she could now see through the outward mask that he kept firmly fixed in place. She'd begun to realise that for much of the time his charming manner was pure fabrication. There were times when she knew he wanted to let the mask slip, but he kept it firmly in place. And at times like that she asked herself why. What did he have to lose? The only answer she could come up with was that he didn't want to lose his integrity by revealing a secret that wasn't his to reveal.

'How is the new prem, Sister?' Simon was asking as his eyes scanned the case-notes on the nurses' station counter.

'Baby Sally is holding up well in her incubator. Her mother is suffering a little discomfort. I told her you'd go and see her when you came in to do your round.'

Simon nodded and turned to look at the medical staff who had hastily assembled at the station counter.

Hannah noticed that the two housemen, James Dewhirst and David Ratcliffe, were obviously feeling the heat as she was, and suffering from lack of sleep. Simon's secretary, Mandy Harrison, was standing, pen poised at the ready, immaculately turned out in an aquamarine linen suit and not a blonde hair out of place. But then, Hannah reminded herself, Mandy got a full night's sleep, so she could manage to look well turned out. A couple of medical students were tagging along. They looked as rumpled as Hannah felt!

'Where's Dr Clarkson?' asked Sister, carefully checking out the members of Simon's entourage, like a teacher calling the register.

'She's in Casualty, looking after a newly admitted threatened miscarriage,' Simon replied. 'We'll start without her.'

The group moved slowly down the ward, chatting to and examining the mothers who had their babies with them before moving on to the prem unit.

Janice Lane, the new prem's mother, appeared a little more comfortable. Simon examined the Caesarean scar and wrote her up for some more pain-killers. Hannah helped Sister to ease the young mother back against her pillows.

'The first day is always the worst, Mrs Lane,' Sister said gently. 'By tomorrow we'll have you up and about, making the tea.'

Janice Lane grimaced. 'As soon as my tummy stops

aching I'll have a lie-in, Sister. How's Sally?'

'Doing fine,' Sister replied. 'You'll be able to go and see her again tomorrow.'

'Why not today?' the mother asked, her hand sweeping over her damp, tousled brown hair.

'I'll arrange for you to be taken in a wheelchair for a few minutes,' Simon said quickly. He turned to look at Sister, who nodded in agreement.

Janice Lane smiled up at Simon. 'You've been so good to me, Doctor.'

Another convert to the fan club! Hannah thought.

Baby Sally was lying on her side in the incubator, wired up to the monitor. Hannah reached through and touched the anterior fontanelle, the small gap between the bones on the baby's head. Although the heartbeat was recorded on the monitor it was always reassuring to feel the steady pulse with some hands-on examination.

'Nothing wrong with Sally's little heart,' she said quietly to Simon.

'Respiration's improving, too,' Simon said.

'How long will you keep the baby on a ventilator, sir?' one of the students asked.

'That will depend entirely on the baby's progress,' Simon replied. 'Each case is different; we read the clinical signs, check the monitor, and make hourly decisions. Better to err on the side of caution with a prem of thirty weeks only, like young Sally here.'

'She's so very tiny,' the student said. 'How much does she weigh?'

'Just two pounds five ounces,' Sister said.

'The mother was suffering from placenta praevia,' Simon continued. 'Like the case we had last month; Madeleine Carter the mother was called. She's already gone home and taken the baby with her to be supervised by the visiting nurses' scheme. I believe you watched that Caesarean, didn't you?'

The student nodded. 'Yes, sir.'

'We've got one case that's causing problems,' Sister put in, moving nearer to Simon. 'Come and advise me about baby Daniel Simpson, the little boy you delivered at the roadside after the car crash. He's two months old now, and fit enough to go home, but his mother keeps ducking the issue. Every time I suggest it, Valerie Simpson says she wouldn't be able to cope.'

Simon looked grave. 'The problem is, I suppose, she's probably spending a lot of time with her husband on the orthopaedics ward. His fractured femur is still in traction, I believe, and. . .'

'I was going to tell you about this case,' Hannah intervened. She'd been waiting to discuss this with Simon for the past couple of days but they'd both been too busy to take on anything else. 'I spoke to the orthopaedic sister and she told me that Valerie Simpson hasn't been in to see her husband for over two weeks.'

Sister frowned. 'So she's avoiding her husband and abandoning her baby.'

'There must be a logical reason,' Hannah put in hurriedly, knowing how stern Sister could be if she felt that any of her mothers weren't shouldering their responsibilities.

They moved on to baby Daniel Simpson's cot at the end of the unit. Hannah stroked Daniel's cheek and he kicked his little legs, as if pleased to have some attention.

'He's a beautiful little boy,' Hannah said, feeling a

lump rising in her throat. How could any mother not want to take this precious infant home? There must be problems she didn't know about in the Simpson household. She touched the silky golden hair on the baby's head.

'Lovely colour.' She turned to look at Simon. 'Shall we see if we can find out if there are some domestic problems?'

Simon nodded and turned to his secretary. 'Get in touch with the social services and see what you can find out. Let me know as soon as possible.'

Mandy Harrison nodded and scribbled in her notebook.

'We can't keep him here much longer. We need the cot,' Sister put in.

'Well, we can't turn him out on the streets,' Simon replied tersely.

Hannah drew in her breath. Simon was losing his self-enforced cool. It was the heat. It must be awful for him, keeping up an outward calm when inwardly he was struggling to come to terms with an impossible situation.

Sister Gregson sniffed in disapproval. 'I'm sure I didn't mean anything of the sort.'

Simon's cool returned and he gave a rueful smile. 'Sorry, Sister, just my little joke. I didn't mean to be taken seriously.'

He recovers pretty quickly, Hannah thought as she watched the smooth demeanour return.

Staff Nurse Rona Phillips was hurrying towards Sister. 'Sorry to interrupt the round, Sister, but there's a man asking if he can see baby Daniel. Says he's a close friend of the family and. . .'

Her voice trailed away as a young man came down the unit, threading his way between the incubators. The first thing that Hannah noticed was the large teddy bear he was carrying. The second thing she observed was the colour of his hair; it was a distinctive golden shade. . .in fact exactly the same shade as baby Daniel's. He'd said he was a friend, but he looked more like a relative.

'I would have preferred you to wait until it was convenient,' Sister began. 'Mr Delaware is in the middle of a round and. . .'

'Don't worry, Sister,' Simon said amiably. 'We can break off for a minute. I'm glad to see someone is taking an interest in little Daniel. You're a friend, I'm told, Mr. . .er. . .?'

'Just a friend of the family,' the man said hurriedly. His eyes were riveted on Daniel as he put the teddy down beside him in the cot. It completely swamped the tiny boy. The man put out his finger and Daniel grasped it, turning blue eyes upwards to look at him.

As the man turned away Hannah saw tears glistening in his eyes.

'His mother asked me to come,' he said huskily. 'She's not well at the moment.'

'Is she well enough to come in and see me?' Hannah said quickly. 'I'm Dr Morgan. She'll remember me.'

The man stared at Hannah for a few seconds. 'I'll try to persuade her,' he said quietly. 'When shall I tell her she can see you, Dr Morgan?'

'Any time,' Hannah said recklessly, knowing that it might ruin her schedule at some point but that this was a problem she couldn't ignore. 'Just come into the hospital and have me paged by the switchboard. I'm out this afternoon, it's my half-day, but. . .'

'I can't contact her for a few days, so it'll be some time next week.'

Hannah felt a mixture of relief and dismay. Relief that she wouldn't have any more commitments piled on her and dismay that it would take so long.

'And you are Mr. . .?' she queried.

He hesitated. 'Colin Archer,' he said, before glancing around him at the watching faces. 'Thanks for everything. Valerie is really ever so grateful.' He took a last look at baby Daniel before striding away down the prem unit.

As Hannah watched him leave she was forming her own theory about Valerie's domestic problems, but she wouldn't express her suspicions until the young mother had been to see her. She desperately wanted to sort out the problem if she could.

At the end of the morning Hannah hurried along the corridor towards the canteen. It was nearly two o'clock and this was supposed to be her half-day. She couldn't wait to get out into the fresh air. But first she had to quell the pangs of hunger. She couldn't even remember the piece of toast she'd washed down with a cup of tea at four that morning after the emergency Caesarean and her tummy was rumbling alarmingly.

'What's the rush? I thought you had a half-day.'

The rumble in her tummy turned to butterflies as she almost collided with Simon coming the other way around the corner of the corridor.

'I *have* got a half-day but I need food first. I'm starving.'

'Could you starve for another few minutes? I've got

one call to make and then I could get some food and
take us on to the moors for a picnic.'

She smiled. 'Sounds good to me. Worth risking death
from starvation.'

'Car park in ten minutes, then?'

She flew back to her room and dragged on a thin
cotton skirt and blouse and flat walking sandals. As
she did so her mind flitted around this unnerving turn
of events. Since that night, when she'd spoken on the
phone to Simon's son, she'd never been alone with
Simon; it had been as if he was at pains to make it
clear that he resented the fact that she'd learned too
much about him.

He seemed to have reinstated his one-date rule with
a vengeance, she'd noticed. He'd obviously discounted
their second date at the farm because it had been
contrived, and the coffee invitation that evening
when they'd both come off duty together must have
been a severely regretted spur of the moment decision.
So, the idea of a picnic together was totally out of
character!

During the past month the hospital grapevine had
been busily discussing a couple of dates that Simon
had made. One was an outing to the flower show at
Ribblestone, near Skipton—Staff Nurse Rona Phillips
had returned in ecstasies from her afternoon out with
the boss, saying how charming and gallant he'd been,
but how he'd never laid a finger on her, worse luck,
and certainly hadn't entertained the idea of taking her
out again.

Then, just last week, Hannah had heard that Simon
had taken theatre sister Margaret Hall out for a meal
at the Coach and Horses. She'd resented the pangs of

jealousy that had shot through her when she'd heard about that evening. But she'd done her best to stifle them because she didn't want to become any more emotionally involved with this mysterious man than she already was.

On the surface, it certainly looked as if Simon liked to play the field. But it was all a façade; she was sure of it. His heart wasn't in these one-date experiences.

So what were his motives today? Was he throwing caution to the winds? she wondered as she went out through the swing doors at the back of the hospital. Or was the heat getting to him? Or was it that. . .?

He was standing beside his silver car, looking remarkably cool in jeans and a cotton shirt, open at the neck. She didn't dare to think about the alternative idea she was formulating because she didn't know how she would feel if he was actually attracted to her. They were simply colleagues spending a few hours together, that was all, she told herself firmly.

Simon drove to the end of the High Street and fed a parking meter, then together they dashed into Marks & Spencer, emerging minutes later with packages of sandwiches, salads, fruit and a bottle of sparkling apple juice. Simon had ruled out the idea of getting a bottle of wine because he said he didn't want to break his drink-drive rule.

'But I could get some wine for you,' he'd told her.

She'd shaken her head, saying that apple juice would be just as thirst-quenching.

She felt the rush of the wind in her hair as Simon drove up the winding road leading on to a moorland fell high above Skipton. The pink of the heather merged with the gold of the gorse bushes to give the effect that the land was aflame.

Simon parked his car at the top of a steep ravine. They gathered up the picnic packages and scrambled down a dusty footpath until they reached a rocky dell where a stream tumbled over glistening stones that sparkled like diamonds in the afternoon sunlight.

Simon spread a car-rug over the bracken and ferns, making a comfortable seat. For several minutes they munched without talking, assuaging their hunger pangs being the first priority.

Hannah lay back against a rock, biting into an apple as she looked up at the cloudless blue sky.

'Mmm, this was such a good idea!' she said. 'What gave you the inspiration?'

'You did,' he replied evenly.

Her heart gave a little jump. She swallowed the piece of apple and closed her eyes against the fierce glare of the sun. For a few seconds the only sound she could hear was the gurgling of the stream, before Simon continued.

'I've decided to abandon my one-date rule. I've been thinking about what you said a couple of months ago, when you first arrived and took on that hilarious bet with Sara. I'm glad you pointed out that everyone had noticed it. So I've come up with another idea.'

She rolled on her side and watched him. He appeared to be searching for exactly the right words. Her heart was now thumping so loudly that if it hadn't been for the babble of the stream she was sure he would have heard it. She waited for him to elaborate on his idea, not knowing how her emotions would react if he wanted to advance their relationship. After all, she knew nothing about his mysterious background. He'd said he wasn't married, but. . .

'I'd like to be able to spend more time with you— a completely platonic relationship with no strings attached. I feel so comfortable with you,' he told her with daunting calm, his enigmatic eyes firmly fixed on her face.

She swallowed. 'A platonic relationship?' she repeated, feeling the dreadful churning of her emotions, the confusion and the disappointment. . . Yes, she was downright disappointed. Nobody had ever described her as comfortable before!

'That's the only relationship I'm free to take on,' he said in a deadpan voice.

'I wish you'd stop being so mysterious and explain why,' she said quietly

He drew in his breath and turned away from her. 'It's quite simple. I'm tired of taking out a different girl for every separate occasion. I need to feel secure in a friendship, to be able to relax as I can with you. Oh, don't worry, I wouldn't make any demands on you. You made it perfectly clear, right from the start, that you're not interested in a deep relationship with me, which is why we could go out together as much as we like without it leading to complications. But if I've offended you by the suggestion. . .'

'You haven't offended me at all,' she burst in, saying the direct opposite of what she was feeling. It hadn't been until he spelled out the idea that she'd realised the true depths of her feelings. Until this moment she'd been deluding herself that she didn't really care.

'But that wasn't what I meant. You haven't explained why you're only free for a platonic relationship. . .not that I'm suggesting that. . .' She paused, drew in her breath and tried again. 'If we're going to spend more time together I'd like you to tell me something about your background. I know you told me you weren't married, but quite frankly. . .'

She broke off as she heard the exasperated intake of his breath. He was lying back against the rock, only inches away from her. She could hear the deep breaths he was taking, presumably to steady his nerves. Minutes passed in silence before he spoke in a flat voice.

'If I'm to tell you, I suppose I'd better start at the beginning. . .I was born in England; my parents divorced when I was very small—I don't remember my father. My mother married an American and we went to live in the States. I studied medicine in Boston. Post-registration I continued to study, came over to London for my fellowship exams, returned to Boston as a consultant. I had lots of girlfriends, but I never thought about marriage. Just never met the right girl. Then six years ago I met Felicity at a party. She was. . .' He paused for breath, plucking a reed and splitting it down the middle before tossing it towards the stream.

Hannah watched the green reed tumbling around in the water, like her own emotions churning away inside her.

'Go on, Simon,' she urged gently. 'Tell me about Felicity.'

He turned towards her and she saw the anguish in his eyes. This was no play-acting. This was the real Simon, stripped of all veneer. Absent-mindedly he reached for her hand and squeezed it gently.

She held herself in check. She was only his friend, his confidante, someone he trusted not to overreach the bounds of that friendship and want more.

'Felicity was in her early twenties, an actress; she was making her way in television commercials, bit-parts in soaps, that sort of thing. She was very temperamental, highly strung, but fun to be with—in small doses. She was very demanding, very jealous, and after a few months of dating her I knew I would have to end our relationship. She was definitely not the girl I wanted to spend the rest of my life with.'

He tugged at a reed growing beside him, his knuckles whitening as he bent it into a knot and hurled it in the air. Hannah waited without speaking.

'On the day I planned to tell her we were finished, she told me she was pregnant. Apparently she'd stopped taking the Pill because she wanted my baby. No, she said, she didn't want to marry me, she just wanted my baby. She was besotted with the idea of having a small child belonging completely to her. She said she'd decided to go home to her widowed mother who had a house near Boston. I insisted I must support my child. She said I could send her monthly cheques but the baby was hers. I tried to keep in touch but she didn't answer my letters or phone calls. In the end I contacted her mother, explained the situation, and she kept me in touch with what was going on.'

He hauled himself to his feet and took a couple of steps towards the stream. Picking up a flat pebble, he skimmed it across the surface of the water until it landed on the far bank. Turning round he fixed tormented eyes on Hannah.

'One month before the baby was due she got drunk,

crashed her car, and went into premature labour. The
baby survived but Felicity was put on a life-support
system. I went to see her in hospital; she was in a
coma. . . Five years on she's still in a coma. Her
mother insists that the life-support system must not be
switched off, even though all medical evidence points
to the fact that Felicity is brain dead.'

He knelt down beside her, slumping back against
the rock, his face a mask of dejection. He reached
again for her hand. Her fingers curled automatically
around his; she could feel the nervous sweat of his
palms as their skin touched.

'What about the baby? Is this Michael, the boy who
phoned when I was in your room?'

He nodded. 'Felicity's mother, Adele, has been
caring for Michael since birth. Minutes after he was
born she convinced me that Michael would be better
off with her than with me. She said I had my career
to think of. She wanted me to be successful so that I
could provide a good home for her daughter when she
came round from the coma. The hospital doctors had
already told us that Felicity was brain dead, but Adele
wouldn't listen. As we sat beside Felicity in those first
few hours she begged me to wait for her daughter,
however long it took. I promised that I would, but at
the same time I made her promise that Michael would
come to live with me if Felicity died. From the prognosis that Felicity's doctors had given me, I didn't think
she would live very long, so my promise to Adele was
to comfort a grieving mother. But as long as she insists
on keeping her daughter on the life-support system
Felicity will linger on, to all intents and purposes
dead. . .but still with a heartbeat. And while she's still

alive Adele has Michael and I must keep my promise to stay free. She lives for her false hopes; I have to respect her feelings and I can't break my promise.'

'But how is it that no one has learned the truth about Felicity?' Hannah asked, her voice strained. Simon's story had moved her to tears. She rubbed the back of her hand across her eyes.

'Her mother didn't want the story to come out in the Press. Felicity was such a tearaway during her teens and her mother doesn't want any more stories printed about her. So I've had to respect her wishes. I've helped her financially to set up a trust fund for Felicity's care. We've jointly poured money into the fund to keep Felicity in a discreet private clinic. But I found the strain of secrecy impossible while I was still working in a nearby hospital. I had to get away and have a life of my own, while keeping Felicity's story secret. That's why I came to Moortown. . .to start this mythical new life. I go back to the States every few months to see Michael. When I go in to see Felicity only a couple of the staff know who I really am now. Felicity's consultant urges me to impress on Adele that there is no hope for Felicity, but she doesn't listen. So you see, as long as Felicity is technically alive, I'm not free. . .'

He turned towards her and pulled her roughly into his arms. She didn't resist when his lips crushed hers in a deeply penetrating kiss.

Moments later he was pulling himself away, his eyes sweeping her face.

'I shouldn't have done that. Not when I'm hoping you'll come out with me more often. . .no strings attached.'

She swallowed hard.

Maybe she should tell him that she'd like a few strings. But she'd only just realised it herself. Better play safe. Better not frighten him away.

A platonic relationship was what they both needed. . .

CHAPTER FIVE

THE heatwave broke as August began, and the fells above Moortown were shrouded in mist as Hannah looked out of her consulting-room window. She was feeling decidedly nervous. It was three weeks since she'd suggested that Valerie Simpson should come in to talk to her and she'd only just received a call from her. The quiet, uncertain voice on the phone half an hour ago had asked for an appointment. Hannah had said, 'Come now,' knowing that with a difficult case like this you had to strike while the iron was hot.

She'd told Simon she would need at least half an hour without interruption and he'd agreed. They'd been in the middle of the morning ward-round on Nightingale when the call had come through.

Mandy Harrison, Simon's secretary had said that the social services had reported that they'd checked on the Simpson family. The report concluded that Valerie and Paul were immature for their nineteen years and unwilling to shoulder responsibility. And there was also the problem of the court case for drinking and driving hanging over Paul Simpson's head when he was discharged from hospital.

Simon had asked if Hannah wanted a professional counsellor to be present during Valerie's appointment, but Hannah thought it might put Valerie off being frank with her. She'd pointed out that she'd spent a lot of time with Valerie while she'd been an in-patient and built up a good, trusting relationship that could well break down if an unknown counsellor was introduced.

There was a knock on the door. Hannah moved quickly to open it.

'Valerie! I'm so glad you got in touch with me.' Hannah smiled down at her diminutive patient, who looked more like a young girl taking a day off school than a mother. 'Come in.'

'There's no need to be so kind. I know what you're all thinking. . .what a lousy mum I am, and you'd be right. Because I don't want that baby. It's not Paul's, you know, so he doesn't want it and. . .'

'Look, sit down, Valerie,' Hannah put in quickly. 'I'm here to help you. I'll do whatever I can if you'll only trust me. Now, you say baby Daniel isn't your husband's baby. Well, you wouldn't be the first person in the world to have that happen to them, you know.'

The young mother stared at Hannah. 'I suppose not, but it feels like it. I never meant it to happen like this. I was going out with Colin. . .he came in to see Daniel, you remember?'

Hannah nodded. 'I remember. Go on, Valerie.'

'I was going out with Colin and we had a row and split up. Then I found I was pregnant with his baby. I was still mad at him so I didn't tell him. I started going out with Paul, and one thing led to another and we got married. When I told him I was pregnant he was pleased. But my dates were all wrong for it to be his and he soon worked that out. On my birthday he took me out to a pub, and when he'd had a few beers he told me he wanted a divorce. Said I'd tricked him into marrying me, which I suppose was true, and he wasn't going to bring up another bloke's kid. I said if that was what he wanted then to go ahead and divorce me. I didn't care. He was real mad when we left the pub, drove like the clappers, and next thing we knew he'd turned the car over and it was going up in flames. God knows what would have happened if that nice doctor hadn't pulled me out. . .'

Hannah drew in her breath as the shock-horror of the situation presented itself again.

'Yes, you were very lucky, Valerie. And lucky to have a beautiful healthy baby.'

The young mother gave a little sob. 'How is Daniel?' she asked in a choking voice.

'He's fine,' Hannah said. She paused, waited, and then plunged straight in. 'He needs you, Valerie; every baby needs a mother. Wouldn't you like to see him?'

'I might. Would he know me?'

'I think he would, but he'll soon forget you if you leave him too long. Oh, there'd be no problem in getting him to transfer his affections to a foster-mother, but. . .'

'I don't want him handing over to a foster-mother,' Valerie said heatedly, as if the full realisation of what might happen had suddenly hit her. 'Yes, I'd like to see him. But I don't want to see Paul. He can have his divorce and marry his girlfriend for all I care.'

'So Paul has a girlfriend?'

Valerie nodded. 'I'm surprised she's not been in to see him, but maybe she doesn't want to get involved. Look here, Dr Morgan, if I take Daniel home with me, will somebody come and show me how to look after him? I don't know anything about babies, and I never had time to go the mother and baby classes.'

'You'll get a great deal of support from the social services, but it would help if you had a relative or friend who could help you.'

'Colin said his mum would help. I always got on well with her. He's told her about the baby and she said I could move in there if Paul was being difficult.'

'Well, that might be a solution,' Hannah said tentatively. She was suddenly deciding that she should have had a professional counsellor from the social services with her, but then maybe Valerie wouldn't have been quite so outgoing. The problem was a complicated one, so she would give a report to the social services and let them take over.

'I'm going to hand your case over to the social services, Valerie. They'll help you make a new life for yourself with Colin and his family if that's what you want.'

'Yes, that's what I want. I love Colin . . . always have.'

Hannah stood up. 'Come and see your lovely baby. He's got Colin's hair, hasn't he?'

Valerie smiled. 'That was the first thing I noticed about him and I thought, Oh my God, what a dead giveaway! But now I'm glad. Colin came back from seeing him and begged me to move in with him and his mum and bring the baby, but I wouldn't. I didn't think I could cope with it all . . . but now I think I can.'

Simon was waiting beside Daniel's cot when Hannah and Valerie arrived. Hannah had made a quick call to make sure that Simon would be there. She wasn't going to take on the responsibility of the case all by herself. There was a lot at stake. She had to be sure that Valerie was capable of handling the new situation.

'Would you like to hold your baby, Valerie?' Simon asked gently.

Baby Daniel smiled up at his mother when she reached down into his cot. At nearly three months, although having been born prematurely, he was normal weight.

'He's lovely, isn't he?' Valerie said, pulling Daniel against her. 'But I still feel scared of looking after him.'

'We'll arrange the support system,' Hannah said. 'Don't worry about it now. We'll look after him until everything is ready for him to go to his new home.'

Seeing the puzzled look on Simon's face, she said, 'I'll explain the situation later. It's going to take some sorting out, but I think we've got a solution.'

The young mother was gazing down at her little son.

It's going to work out, Hannah was trying to convince herself. Between the social services, the hospital medical staff, and Colin and his mother, baby Daniel would be well provided for. She would also arrange for a professional counsellor to visit Paul and give him some help and support.

Valerie thanked Simon and Hannah and made off down the ward, glancing back several times for a glimpse of her son.

'Let me explain what's going on,' Hannah said.

'Not now,' Simon said a trifle brusquely. 'I didn't want to hurry you but I'm due in Theatre. Emergency ectopic. Sara has done the preparation but I'd like you to assist me now.'

Arriving at Theatre One, Hannah found the team were ready and waiting, and the patient already anaesthetised on the table.

Simon incised the abdomen and ligated the bleeding

points before removing the affected Fallopian tube containing the remains of the tubal pregnancy.

'First pregnancy for this patient,' Simon said as he worked, explaining what he was doing for the benefit of the watching students. 'Statistics show that tubal pregnancies occur in the ratio of about one in one hundred and fifty. They happen because some factor has slowed the progress of the egg through the Fallopian tube. Sometimes this is the result of fibrosis, or we could have a congenital abnormality of the tube, or the egg might have crossed from the ovary to the opposite tube across the pelvic cavity. Our patient here, Jill Courtney, was in considerable pain when admitted with a high temperature and bleeding from the vagina. As you can see here, the tube had almost ruptured.'

Hannah swabbed the area where Simon was working. She was thinking that it would have been much worse if the tube had ruptured. As it was, the patient should make a full recovery and be able to conceive again, having one perfectly intact tube left.

After Simon had sutured the abdominal wound, Hannah went back to the ward with their patient and arranged for a nurse to special her. She changed the IV from a saline infusion to blood, now that the patient had been grouped and cross-matched.

'Mrs Courtney,' she said gently as the patient began to come round.

'Where am I?' the patient whispered.

Simon had just arrived at the bedside from Theatre and he was leaning over the patient as he checked the IV. 'You're in hospital, Mrs Courtney. Would you. . .?'

'Did I lose it?' the patient interrupted hoarsely.

'I'm afraid so,' Simon said gently.

Jill Courtney closed her eyes. 'Didn't know I was pregnant until I came in. Thought I'd got appendicitis or something.'

'You had what we call an ectopic pregnancy,' Hannah said. 'The egg was fertilised in the Fallopian tube.'

'Funny how you can get attached to the idea of being a mum in just a few minutes. I think I'll go back to sleep.'

Hannah walked with Simon to the door. 'She's going to be all right,' Simon said. 'It always hits them hard when this happens.'

Hannah nodded. Try as she would, she always felt sad when a patient lost a potential baby.

They walked down the corridor without speaking, each deep in thought. Hannah broke the silence by discussing the Valerie and Paul Simpson case.

Simon nodded in agreement with the decisions Hannah had made. 'I'll ask Mandy to follow up those ideas. If Colin's mother agrees to take Valerie and the baby in, that would be a good solution. But then Paul is going to need counselling, especially with his drink-driving case coming up when he gets out of hospital.'

He paused and put a hand on her arm. 'Now, how about some lunch?'

'Love some,' Hannah said. 'The canteen shouldn't be too crowded at this time.'

'I'm not talking about the canteen. I'd like to drive out of town. Want to come?'

'Why not?' she replied, thinking that, although three weeks ago he'd said he wanted to see more of her, he'd made no attempt to fix a date. She'd come to the conclusion that he'd regretted the fact that she knew about his background. Perhaps he'd been waiting to see if he could really trust her to keep a secret.

The rain was tearing down in sheets, splattering the windscreen. Hannah felt snug and cosy huddled up on the passenger seat.

'I want to try a new restaurant,' Simon said. 'It's a bit far out but worth the journey, so I'm told.'

'You mean you haven't taken anyone there before?' Hannah said with mock-surprise. 'That's unusual.'

Simon gave a wry grin. 'I've always spread my dates around the area. Never take more than one girl to the same restaurant.'

'Of course not. It would confuse the restaurant staff.'

She was surprised at the bitterness she felt and was careful to conceal it with a light-hearted, carefree tone of voice.

They drove on, the silence broken only by the purr of the engine and the constant thud of rain on the windscreen.

'My, my, this looks posh,' Hannah said as they pulled into the gravelled forecourt of an Elizabethan manor-house. 'Doesn't look like a restaurant. Are you sure. . .?'

'It's one of those places where the owner likes to create the ambience of a private lunch or dinner party. I read about it in one of the good food guides.'

Hannah ran across the gravel while Simon tried to shield them both with his umbrella. A waiter greeted them in the porch.

'Let me take your umbrella, sir. If you would like to walk this way. . .'

They were ushered into a high-ceilinged, oak-panelled room with a huge log fire blazing at one end. The waiter brought them drinks as they sat in comfortable armchairs, either side of the fireplace, and handed over large, glossy-fronted menus.

The menu ran into several pages. Hannah cast her eyes over it and chose Dover sole followed by turkey in a blue cheese sauce.

They were served at a small table in a bay window overlooking the rain-drenched countryside. Hannah looked out at the low-lying clouds over the fells, feeling cosseted by her luxuriously cosy surroundings.

Deliberately, they kept their conversation away from hospital topics. Once, when Hannah brought up the subject of the Simpson family, she stopped in mid-sentence.

'It can wait,' she said.

Simon reached across the starched white linen table-cloth and squeezed her hand. 'I should hope it can,' he said quietly.

She felt the now-familiar churning of her emotions as she realised that if only they could get on with their own lives. . .

The waiter was standing by the table with plates of fresh strawberries and cream. Simon removed his hand.

'Delicious!' Hannah whispered as they returned to their seats beside the fire to sip coffee from delicate bone china cups. 'I don't mind sharing a platonic relationship when you bring me out to places like this.'

She saw a shadow cross his face.

'It's good to have someone I can confide in,' he said huskily.

She remained very still, the silence broken only by the sound of the logs crackling on the fire.

'I'm never free of this overwhelming feeling of responsibility to Felicity and Michael, but since I met you——'

He broke off as a waiter reappeared, asking if he could get anything for them.

'A brandy, perhaps, sir?'

'Not when I'm driving,' Simon replied firmly.

'I'll drive,' Hannah said.

Simon gave her a wry grin. 'Do you think you can handle my car?'

'Of course I can! I can handle most machines,' she replied. 'It can't be any more difficult than my battered old Ford. I'm dying to get my hands on it.'

'OK.' He turned to the waiter. 'Yes, I'll have a Remy Martin.'

Hannah watched him relaxing as he leaned back against the high-backed chair, swirling the brandy in his glass as he gazed into the flames.

'One of the reasons I have this strict rule about drinking and driving is because of Felicity,' he said quietly. 'If she hadn't got drunk that day, she would still be a normal woman.'

'And would you still be in touch with her if she wasn't on a life-support machine?' Hannah asked gently.

The question seemed to take him off-guard. 'Never really thought about it. I suppose I would have to see her because of Michael. But I wouldn't be seeing her because I wanted to. If Adele hadn't extracted that promise from me about keeping myself free for Felicity I would have broken all contact with her.'

He gave a deep sigh and closed his eyes, as if remembering the exact moment five years before.

'It was only minutes after Michael was born. Felicity's doctors had told me she wouldn't live very long. Adele was hysterical. She said all she'd wanted when she knew her daughter was pregnant was for Felicity and the baby and me to be together as a family. She knew we'd had our differences—what an understatement!—but she'd hoped and prayed for a reconciliation, so if I didn't want to break her heart I had to promise to marry Felicity as soon as she came round from the coma. I agreed. . .because I knew it wouldn't happen. . .'

He paused, running a hand through his thick dark hair in exasperation.

'I know I have to keep my side of the bargain so that eventually I can have Michael to live with me. . .I suppose that sounds harsh.'

'No, it doesn't. Just truthful.'

A waiter was filling up her coffee-cup. She leaned back in her chair and watched as Simon fought to control the deep emotions that the impossible situation aroused. If they hadn't been in the middle of a restaurant she would have reached out and put her arms around him. He'd said it was good to confide in her and she knew he needed comfort; oh, he was still the big, strong, successful consultant, but underneath he was desperately vulnerable, torn in two by a problem that couldn't be resolved.

'Tell me about Michael,' she said, after a few moments had elapsed and they were alone again.

She saw a happy smile appear on his face and felt a warm glow deep inside her. He was every inch the proud father as he began to talk.

'He's very bright for a five-year-old. . .' He turned to look at Hannah and she smiled back at him.

'But, of course. That goes without saying, if he's your son. I expect he's a genius.'

Simon laughed. It was a good, genuine sound, not the brittle, contrived laughter he sometimes affected.

'You should laugh like that more often,' Hannah said.

He pulled his chair nearer, shortening the gap between them.

'Go on, tell me more about Michael,' she said.

He took another sip of brandy. 'His hair is dark like mine. He can be a little scamp but he's very loving and——' He broke off. 'One day I hope you'll meet him,' he said huskily. 'Now, we've got the rest of the afternoon free. We don't need to be back until this evening—the hospital will call me on the mobile if anything comes up. I'd like you to come and look over a house with me.'

'A house? Are you thinking of buying a place?'

He gave her a wry grin. 'It has been known for consultants approaching forty to invest some of their savings in property. Yes, I've decided I ought to have a place of my own. When, eventually, I can have Michael with me, I'm going to need somewhere for him to live.' He paused. 'And someone to look after him.'

She stared at him, her pulse quickening, waiting for him to elaborate, but when he did it was in a matter-of-fact tone; there was nothing remotely romantic about the situation.

'I've found a house in Cragdale which sounds as if it might be the right place; it's only a few minutes by car from Moortown and comes with a resident house-keeper.'

'That's unusual. . .the housekeeper, I mean.'

'Well, apparently the owner of the house is a widow who's finding it difficult to make ends meet, so she's put the house on the market on the proviso that she can live in part of the house and work as housekeeper. The house comprises three sixteenth-century cottages all made into one; the housekeeper would live at one end and the new owner would live in the remaining two cottages.'

'I know Cragdale,' Hannah said. 'A pretty little village it is. I suppose it could be an advantage having a resident housekeeper; on the other hand. . .'

'Oh, I wouldn't contemplate it if I didn't think the owner would be suitable for Michael. He's my number one priority. So I thought you would help me sort that one out. Two heads are better than one, and you being a woman. . . Anyway, I've actually got an appointment at the house in half an hour.'

Hannah smiled. 'So this lunch was to put me in the right mood, so that I would give you some free advice, was it?'

He laughed. 'Something like that. Partly business but mostly pleasure.'

She hauled herself reluctantly out of her chair.

Simon stood in front of her, looking down at her with an enigmatic expression in the flickering firelight. She noticed how the cleft in his chin reached the edge of his full, sensuous lower lip. Already the dark hairs were showing on his chin. He was obviously one of those swarthy men who needed to shave twice a day. She was beginning to know him so well. . .to feel something for him akin to love. . . Yes, she admitted to herself reluctantly, she was falling in love with a man caught in a situation that prevented him from reciprocating her feelings. . .

She turned away and looked towards the ancient mullioned windows, set deep in the thick stone walls. Outside, the dark sky glowered. Hannah felt an overwhelming desire to stay on in this limbo land of no decisions.

Simon put out his hand and she took it, feeling a stir of excitement as their fingers touched.

'Let's go,' he said quietly. 'Got to get back to the real world.'

She smiled up at him. 'You felt it too, didn't you? We were cocooned away from reality.'

He nodded. 'We can come back. . .some time. . .'

'I'd like that,' she whispered, almost to herself.

As Simon had described, it was a rambling, sixteenth-century house, made up of three cottages, beside the river that flowed through Cragdale. Hannah manoeuvred the silver sports car until they were only yards from the front porch.

'You're not such a bad driver,' Simon said as she pulled on the handbrake.

'That's a rather grudging compliment,' she said. 'Why don't you add that I'm not such a bad driver for a woman?'

He laughed. 'Because I don't make sexist remarks.'

'I'm glad to hear it!'

They made a dash through the rain and struck on the brass doorknocker.

A woman of about fifty opened the thick oak door and stood back so that they could run inside.

'Terrible weather!' she said. 'I'm Dorothy Rainer and you must be Mr Delaware. Let me take your coats. Would you like some tea?'

They said they would love some, after they'd seen the house.

'Mrs Rainer, this is Dr Hannah Morgan,' Simon said.

The older woman smiled welcomingly. 'Just wander round and come into the sitting-room when you're ready.'

'She seems very nice,' Hannah whispered as they climbed the narrow staircase to the first floor. 'Do you know if she was recently widowed?'

'Her husband died last year, I believe. She's putting the house and contents up for sale. That would suit me fine, because I don't want the hassle of having to furnish a place from scratch. I can add my own things as I go along.'

'There are some lovely antiques.' Hannah ran her fingers over a well-polished Chippendale settee nestling in the corner of the long landing. 'And a four-poster bed in the master bedroom. Simon, it's superb!'

She turned to find him standing behind her. He held out his arms, and without a word she went into the warm circle of his embrace. Her heart fluttered as she raised her face towards him. He bent his head and their lips met briefly before he pulled away and moved towards the staircase.

She followed him, thinking that it had been an impulsive kiss on his part; she mustn't read anything into it.

'The floor slopes alarmingly!' she cried. 'It's like being on board a ship in a storm. It would be such fun to live here. . .'

She stopped as he turned to look at her. He was smiling, obviously pleased by her enthusiasm, but she felt she was going too far—making it plain that she would love to live here.

But that wasn't on the cards. This was the house where Simon would install his son. . .when the time came, whenever that might be. She had no part in this venture other than as a confidential adviser and friend.

They went down to the ground floor. Mrs Rainer was serving tea in the sitting-room: scones, cream, home-made raspberry jam; tea from a porcelain teapot, logs on the open fire.

'It's idyllic here,' Simon said, declining a second scone.

Mrs Rainer smiled. 'That's not what potential clients should be saying. I expected you to find fault with things so as to bring the price down.'

'If it's what I want I won't quibble over the price,' Simon said. 'I need a place to bring my five-year-old son when. . .when he comes to live with me. He's in the States with his grandmother. It may not be for some time yet. . .in fact it could be years. So, how would you feel about having a young boy here, Mrs Rainer?'

'I love children. My daughter is grown-up and married now, so I'd enjoy helping you to look after your son. . .if you decide to take the house. Will you be moving in too, Dr Morgan?'

'No. I'm just a colleague of Mr Delaware's,' Hannah put in quickly.

'Forgive me. . .I thought. . .'

'I came to offer advice,' Hannah said, firmly avoiding Simon's eyes.

'So what would you advise, Hannah?' Simon asked evenly.

'I think it's perfect!'

'Well, then, all we've got to do is sort out the financial side,' Simon said.

The soft tonal sound of Simon's mobile phone disturbed them.

'Excuse me,' he murmured. 'Yes? OK. . .I'll be there in a few minutes. Set up the theatre. Yes, I'll contact Dr Morgan. . .'

He put the phone back in his pocket. 'We've got an emergency Caesarean. Sorry to have to rush off, Mrs Rainer. My solicitor will be in touch with you.'

Mrs Rainer waved them off as they ran through the rain to the car.

'I'll drive,' Simon said. 'It's over an hour since that brandy and I've drunk gallons of tea. You really do like the house, don't you?'

'I love it!' Hannah turned round to get a last glimpse.

'Do you think Michael will like it? And will he like Mrs Rainer?'

'Yes to both questions.'

'It will be a dream come true when I can have Michael there with me.'

Hannah noticed the whitening of his knuckles on the steering-wheel.

'When will you move in?'

'As soon as the solicitors sort out the necessary paperwork. There's nothing to hold me back. . . Now, about this Caesarean we're going to do. . .'

She leaned back against the chair, knowing that the pleasure side of the afternoon was over. Simon was once more the experienced consultant, intent on performing a skilful operation. He seemed to find it easier than she did to switch from the personal side of his life to the professional. But then, she reminded herself, he'd had more practice than she had.

She took a deep breath as she mentally readjusted to their becoming consultant and registrar again.

The theatre was already prepared for them. The patient, a twenty-five-year-old woman in her third pregnancy, had been in labour for a couple of hours in her own home. The midwife had called an ambulance when she'd realised that the breech presentation of the foetus was impossible to correct.

'This is Mrs Sylvia Whitfield,' Simon told the students as he made the first incision.

Hannah swabbed the bleeding and stood back again to watch Simon as he worked his way through the outer abdominal layer of tissue.

'As you can see, she's chosen to have an epidural anaesthetic so that she can be awake when her baby is born.'

'Can she feel anything, sir?' one of the students asked.

'No, I can't,' came the muffled reply from the patient.

Hannah could see that Simon was smiling behind his mask.

'You're an absolutely model patient, Mrs Whitfield,' he said.

'Well, it is my third baby, so I've had a lot of practice. I'd wanted to have this one at home, but the little blighter decided to be difficult.'

'It's not so little, Sylvia,' Simon said. 'Tell me about your other babies. Boys or girls?'

'Two boys, so I'm hoping for a girl.'

Simon was cutting through the uterine wall and extricating a slippery baby.

'You're in luck. It *is* a girl!'

A chorus of 'Ahh!' went round the theatre. Hannah looked across the table and her eyes met Simon's. For a second he was stripped of all pretence, before he turned to speak to the students again with the extrovert, play-to-the-gallery charm they all loved. He looked like a man without a care in the world.

If they only knew! Hannah thought.

CHAPTER SIX

DURING the month of September Hannah had a rapid turnover of patients in the obstetrics section of Nightingale Wing. She was relieved that there were only a few complicated cases requiring periods of long stay, but at the same time it meant that Hannah barely had time to get to know the mothers before they were discharged.

But in the babies' section, off the prem unit, there were still several long-stay cases. On the morning that baby Daniel Simpson was due to go home, Sister Gregson telephoned Hannah in the middle of her outpatient clinic.

'Mrs Simpson has arrived to take her baby Daniel home, Dr Morgan. You asked me to let you know when she arrived.'

'Thanks, Sister. I'll come up now,' Hannah said.

Fortunately, one patient had just gone out and the next hadn't been called in.

'I'll be ten minutes,' she told Staff Nurse Rona Phillips.

Hurrying down Nightingale Wing, she saw a group gathered around Daniel Simpson's cot. Valerie Simpson was sitting on the bedside chair dressing her little son in a brand new outfit of blue dungarees and sweater.

'He looks more than four and a half months old, doesn't he, Dr Morgan?' Valerie said proudly. 'Who would have thought he'd have grown this big?'

Hannah looked around at the people with the young mother. She smiled at Colin Archer, with his fiery golden hair, so obviously the proud father.

'This is my mum, Doctor,' he said, introducing a cheery-looking plump lady.

All Hannah's doubts about the situation were dispelled as she shook hands with Mrs Archer. She was just the sort of motherly woman who would be a great help to Valerie.

'I'm glad it's all turned out for the best, Doctor,' Mrs Archer said. 'They never should have split up, these two, in the first place. I said all along that Valerie was a fool to marry that Paul Simpson. Now they've got all the bother of going through a divorce.'

'It's just a formality, Mum,' Colin said quickly. 'Don't worry about it. I've talked to Paul about it and he won't stand in our way.'

'So you've been in contact with Paul, have you?' Hannah said. This was something the social services didn't know about. They'd been keeping her in touch with the case. She'd also been getting weekly reports from Paul's counsellor. He'd been discharged from hospital a couple of weeks before but the counselling had continued at his request. He'd received a suspended prison sentence for the drink-driving offence. The judge had said he would definitely have sent him straight to prison if he hadn't been so badly injured. But he'd warned him that a further offence would activate the suspended sentence, regardless of his condition.

'I went to see him at home, when he came out of hospital,' Colin said. 'His girlfriend was already living there, looking after him, so he didn't cause me any problems. There were no hard feelings on either side, really.'

'Well, that's a relief,' Hannah said. 'All ready now, Valerie? I'm going to miss your beautiful little boy. You'll bring him back to the clinic won't you?'

''Course I will. Thanks for everything, Dr Morgan.'

Hannah hurried back to Outpatients, feeling satisfied that this case could now be closed as far as she was concerned. But it could so easily have been a complete tragedy if Simon hadn't been there when Paul Simpson crashed his car.

A couple of hours and ten patients later, she switched off her computer and moved out into the main outpatient hall to go for lunch.

The canteen was busy as she carried her tray over to join Sarah Clarkson, who had a foursome table all to herself.

Hannah put her vegetable soup and tuna salad on the table.

'I'm curious to know how you're getting on with the boss,' Sara said. 'Rumour has it that you've been seeing a lot of each other.'

'Well, we do happen to work in the same department,' Hannah replied, not looking up from her soup.

Sara laughed. 'That's not what I mean and you know it! So what can you tell me about our mystery man?'

'Nothing—absolutely nothing. He's a very private person, as you well know.'

'Yes, but you must have found out something about him. You've been here nearly five months.'

Hannah didn't reply.

Sara tried again. 'I notice he's stopped taking other

people out. You seem to be his constant companion, as they say in newspaper jargon.'

'And, in newspaper jargon, we're just good friends.' Sara laughed. 'Pull the other one!'

Again, Hannah didn't reply. She wasn't going to divulge anything to Sara. . .or anyone else for that matter.

'Well, how about the rumour that he's buying a house? You must know something about that?'

'Could well be true. After all, a man has to live somewhere, and it's a bit cramped in the residents' quarters.'

'So he's planning to settle down, is he?'

'I really wouldn't know what he's planning,' Hannah said, putting her knife and fork down in the middle of her salad. Suddenly her appetite had gone. 'Excuse me, I'm in a hurry,' she said, and she made for the outer door and the anonymity of the car park.

It was true that she was in a hurry. She'd been promising her mother she'd pop over for a few hours as soon as she could find the time. Her car fired on the first turn of the key.

'Wonders never cease!' she said under her breath. Her ancient car had been playing up recently and she knew she would have to sort out her finances and buy a newer one soon. But while it still ran she was going to keep this one. She'd had it since she was a student and was attached to it, even if the red paint was chipped and the engine going rusty.

'Keep on like this, old dear,' she said as her car rattled out through the car park, 'and I won't be putting you out to grass.'

She held back to let an ambulance tear through the

hospital gates and then she was out on the road, heading towards the Moortown ring road.

Suddenly it occurred to her that she could make a
slight detour to have another look at Simon's house.
She presumed the sale was going through, but he
hadn't mentioned it to her since last month when they'd
been out there together.

Turning off the ring road, she took the road that
led down into Cragstone village. She drove over the
humpback bridge in the centre of the village and
brought the car to a halt beside the river. Upstream,
the old house looked cosy and inviting in the late summer sunshine. Hannah felt a jolt of emotion as she
looked at it. This was where Simon was going to bring
his son when. . .

'Hannah!'

She turned. Simon was striding over from the
direction of the village store.

'What are you doing here?' he asked.

'I was on my way to see my parents. Thought I'd
make a detour and have another look at the house.'

'The sale's going through. I should be able to move
in next month. Mrs Rainer has been so helpful.'

'You're very lucky to find a house and a housekeeper.'

'The other day she asked me when I was going to
bring my son over. I had to tell her it might be years,
but I didn't explain why and she was too polite to ask
any more questions.'

'I hope Michael's not grown-up before he comes to
live with you.'

He put a hand on her arm. 'You sound bitter.'

'Realistic would be more correct. Are you prepared

to wait while Michael's childhood slips away?'

She was alarmed by the pain in his expression.

'I'm sorry; I had no right to say that,' she put in hurriedly.

'I suppose you think I should apply for custody through the courts,' he said in a cool tone. 'But I don't want Michael turned into one of those tug-of-love kids. I prefer to stick to an amicable agreement with Adele.'

'I didn't mean to interfere,' Hannah said quickly, turning away from Simon. Her eyes were drawn once again to the pretty cottage by the stream.

'Would you like to look round the house again?' he asked, obviously aware that he'd upset her and anxious to make amends. 'I'm sure Mrs Rainer would. . .'

'Haven't time. I promised my parents I'd go over.'

He took hold of her by the shoulders, his fingers firm but infinitely disturbing. 'I'd like to go with you. I've got a couple of hours free and I enjoyed my visit last time.'

She stared at him, an alarmed expression creeping unwittingly over her face. 'Are you sure? My mother will give you the third degree, you know.'

'I can handle your mother's interrogation, except. . .' He paused. 'You haven't told her anything about me, have you?'

'Absolutely not! Which is why she'll jump to the wrong conclusion when I turn up with you for the second time.'

'Not if we make it look like a platonic relationship,' he said, his eyes unflickering as they looked down on her.

She met his gaze. 'Which is what it is, isn't it?'

'Of course.' He turned away.

Hannah couldn't see the expression he was hiding but she could hear his deep breathing.

'We'll take my car,' he said. 'Leave yours here in the lay-by. We'll collect it on the way back.'

Gwen Morgan was over the moon when Simon drove his shining silver sports car through the farmyard gates.

'What a lovely surprise! It's been months since you were here. I kept saying to Hannah, "When are you going to bring Simon over to see us again?"'

Hannah held back, hoping her mother wasn't going to embarass her by planting a kiss on Simon's cheek.

She breathed a sigh of relief as her father appeared at the kitchen door and took charge of Simon.

'Come and see the new bantam chicks I've just bought while the girls get the tea ready.'

Simon went willingly across the farmyard towards the south-facing field, where ten fluffy little chickens were scratching around the henhouse in the warm afternoon sunlight.

'Bought them at the market in Skipton last Saturday. There's nothing like. . .'

Hannah could hear the sound of her father's excited voice as she followed her mother into the kitchen.

'And about time too! Where have you been hiding him all these weeks?'

'Mum, there's nothing going on between Simon and me. We're just good friends,' she said, aware that it was the second time she'd said that in the space of a few hours. Was anybody taken in by it, least of all herself?

'Oh, come on, Hannah, I wasn't born yesterday!

I've only got to see the way you look at each other to know. . .'

'Mum, you're wrong! You mustn't say things like that. . .especially in front of Simon. He. . .there are problems, and. . .'

'He's not married, is he? Better not be. If he's married, you mustn't have anything to do with him. Nice as he is, get out while you can. There's no future in an affair with a married man. Why, I've known. . .'

'Mum, he's not married!' Hannah realised her voice was raised. She reached up into the kitchen cupboard by the sink for the flowered cups and saucers. The bottom saucer dropped from the pile and smashed on the draining-board.

'I'm sorry, Mum,' she said in a small voice.

'That's all right, love. I can see you're not yourself today. Been working too hard, haven't you?'

Gwen Morgan had already reached for the dustpan and brush and was busily removing the broken pieces.

'I can see it's not all plain sailing between you and Simon, so. . .'

'There's nothing going on, Mum. Please forget I said there were problems, because. . .'

The door opened and the two men came in.

'Oh, had a little accident, have we?' said her father cheerily. 'Well, never mind, worse things happen at sea. Come through to the sitting-room, Simon.'

'If ever you need a shoulder to cry on, love,' her mum said softly as she dumped the pieces in the waste-bin, 'remember, I'm the one who used to patch you up when you fell down and scratched your little knees. Just because you're grown-up it doesn't mean you can handle everything that life throws at you. So remember, I'm here if. . .'

'Thanks, Mum,' Hannah said. Watching her mother's tight-lipped face she knew she'd convinced herself that Simon was married. And there wasn't a thing she could do to convince her otherwise. Not without giving away a secret that she'd sworn not to reveal.

The tea and cakes in the sitting-room were served in a decidedly strained atmosphere. Gareth Morgan did his best to defuse the situation but Hannah could see he was dying to get Gwen to himself and ask her what the matter was.

The shrilling of Simon's mobile phone was almost a relief. Hannah found herself hoping they would have to leave immediately and go back to hospital.

'Yes, I'll come at once,' Simon said, after listening intently for a few seconds.

Hannah stood up. 'Was it the hospital?'

Simon nodded. 'The porter's lodge with a message. I'll have to go over to the States.' He glanced around at the enquiring faces. 'A family problem.'

Hannah saw the look on her mother's face—the look of 'I told you so'.

'Anything I can do?' Hannah asked, her spirits plummeting.

'You'd better come back to hospital so I can brief you on taking charge while I'm away.'

Gwen Morgan was on her feet moving towards the door, being distantly polite as she showed her guest out. Gareth Morgan was shaking hands with Simon, still unsure what this was all about.

'Don't forget to phone, Hannah!'

Her mother's voice echoed down the lane.

'Why was your mother so cool with me?' Simon asked as he negotiated the bend that put the farm out of sight of the lane.

'I just happened to say that you had problems. She jumped to conclusions and she's convinced herself you're married.'

'Might as well be,' he muttered grimly. 'Adele is breathing down my neck again. Demanding that I go immediately to Boston. I have to go; it could be she's seen the light and decided to let the doctors switch off the support system, in which case. . .'

He reached across and took hold of her hand. She held her breath as the full implication hit her.

'You would be free, wouldn't you, Simon?' she breathed.

'Free to live my own life again,' he said quietly.

The car was purring down the hill towards Cragdale. He pulled into a widened part of the lane and switched off the engine, staring straight ahead through the wind-screen at the narrow road which meandered down the valley between ancient, roughly built walls.

'Felicity has been dead to me for so long, it would be hypocritical of me to mourn,' he said. 'I'm sad that we had such a traumatic relationship, but if she was to be allowed to come off the life-support system after all these years——'

He broke off and reached across towards Hannah. 'I can't even put it into words,' he said as he pulled her into his arms. 'It's as if I'm being disloyal if I say how I feel about you,' he said softly against her hair.

She remained still, until he cupped her face in his hands and gently, oh, so gently, kissed her on the lips.

The butterflies in her stomach danced madly: her spine tingled with excitement and longing for something more. She wanted the passions welling up inside her to develop into a full-blown sensual experience. Confined here in her cramped seat, she wanted so much to lose herself in a long, passionate embrace.

'I must go,' he whispered. 'There's so much to do before I can leave for the airport tonight.'

'Tonight?' she echoed, feeling something akin to panic.

'Don't worry. You'll be able to cope with the hospital work,' he said, pulling himself away.

She straightened up in her seat as he restarted the engine. Oh, yes, she'd cope with the hospital work. It was her own impossible emotions that would be the problem while he was away.

For two weeks, Hannah was in charge of the Delaware firm. She knew she could call on Horace Dixon, the consultant of the other obstetrics and gynaecology firm, if there was something she couldn't handle, but in the event she found she could cope. Her junior staff rose to the occasion and were very supportive.

It was only the constant questions from her colleagues that threatened to get her down. In particular, Sara was becoming more and more inquisitive.

Coming off duty together, towards the end of the second week, Sara persuaded Hannah to have a coffee with her.

Curled up in the corner of an armchair in Sara's room, she closed her eyes as she sipped.

'You must be exhausted,' Sara said. 'Doing Simon's

work as well as your own. When is he coming back from the States?'

'I've no idea,' Hannah replied.

She was glad she didn't have to lie. In two weeks she'd heard nothing from him, not even a phone call. On the previous night she'd lain awake, wondering if Felicity was already dead, and had felt the most awful pangs of guilt at hoping the life-support system had been switched off. She'd had to convince herself again that it would be the most sensible course of action. Felicity was brain dead. There was no point in prolonging her life.

Sara's phone rang.

'Dr Clarkson here. . . Yes, Dr Morgan is with me at the moment. Would you like. . .? Oh, I see. . .'

Sara put the phone down and faced Hannah. 'There's a person to person call for you. . .from the States. They're putting it through to your room, apparently. Not difficult to guess who that might be on the other end.'

Hannah ignored Sara's curiosity as she leapt to her feet. Her pulses were racing as she rushed from the room. Yes, it could only be Simon. . . And would the news be that he was now free, and if so would he. . .?

'Simon?' She gripped her phone as her voice came out in a breathless rush.

'How did you know it was me?'

She gave a nervous laugh. 'Who else would be calling from the States, person to person?'

'I want you to do something for me.'

She held her breath, knowing that at that moment she would have done anything for him. Please let it be. . .

'I want you to go over to my house and alert Mrs
Rainer to the fact that I'm bringing Michael home with
me. We want to move in next week. I haven't yet
explained my situation to her and you're the only
person who can do that. But you'll have to be discreet.
I don't want a whisper of Felicity's story to reach the
Press. So long as she's still on the life-support system,
we have to keep the story secret.'

Hannah swallowed, guilt-ridden by the conflicting
emotions that threatened to overcome her. So the situation hadn't changed.

'Are you still there, Hannah?'

'Yes, I was wondering how you'd managed to persuade Adele to let you have Michael.'

'I was coming to that. Adele has just got married
to someone she's known for years—an old friend of
her husband's. He'd been asking her for some time
and she finally decided she would say yes. Adele is in
her fifties; Tom, her new husband, in his sixties. The
reason Adele asked me to come out, apart from
attending the wedding, was because Tom wanted to
take her on a two-month honeymoon cruise and he
didn't want to have to take Michael along. Of course
I said I would be delighted to bring Michael back to
England with me.'

'So, he'll just be with you for two months? All this
to-ing and fro-ing isn't going to be very good for
him, is it?'

As soon as she'd spoken she knew Simon would
think she was interfering again.

'So what would you suggest?' he asked evenly. 'You
know the situation; there's no solution as long as
Felicity is technically alive.'

'I agree; it's an impossible situation,' she said quickly. 'Has there been any change in Felicity's condition?'

'None at all. Adele is still convinced she will recover, so nothing has changed there. Felicity's doctors tell me she could go on living for years if she remains on the life-support system.'

Hannah drew in her breath. Deep down, the hopes of the last two weeks were crumbling away. She could see years and years stretching ahead, during which she would be Simon's confidante—or dogsbody, whichever way you liked to look at it. Yes, he had problems— he was in an impossible situation—but he couldn't expect her to wait around, dancing to his tune, shredding herself emotionally and physically by dwelling on a dream that didn't look as if it would ever come true.

'I'll go to see Mrs Rainer,' she said in a calm voice that belied her inner turmoil. 'I'll explain the situation and the necessity for secrecy. When exactly shall I tell her you propose to move in?'

'Thursday afternoon. I've told the powers that be I'll be back in hospital on Friday. But I needed you to speak to Mrs Rainer for me. It's not the sort of situation you can explain over the phone. You're sure you don't mind?'

'Not at all,' she said, feeling exactly the opposite as she told herself that after she'd finished this diplomatic mission to see Mrs Rainer she would put an end to their charade of a relationship. She couldn't be there every time Simon needed her. The futility of it was tearing her apart.

'Hannah, are you still there?'

She took a deep breath. 'Yes, I've got to go now,

Simon. I need some sleep before I get called out again. It's tough doing two jobs.'

'I know, and I'm truly grateful. I'll make it up to you when I come back.'

She steeled herself against the caressing tones of his voice.

'I've missed you so much, Hannah. I can't wait to be with you again.'

His voice was even more tender. She could imagine his dark hair falling over his forehead, his high-cheekboned aristocratic features softening as he spoke to her, the cleft in his chin that rubbed against her when they kissed. . .

'Goodnight, Simon,' she said, and rammed the phone back on the cradle.

Seconds later the tears ran down her cheeks. She brushed at them viciously with a tissue.

She got up from her chair and crossed to her little shower-room. As the water cascaded over her naked body she tried to convince herself that it was over.

CHAPTER SEVEN

SIMON'S house by the river in Cragdale was shrouded in morning mist as Hannah parked her car on the wide gravel drive surrounded by the damp lawn. It was the first day of October and there was a definite autumnal nip in the air. She climbed out and made her way over the leaf-strewn path to the front door.

Impressive for a cottage door, she thought as she grasped the well-polished brass doorknocker. There had been many alterations to the basic three cottages, but the ancient character of the place remained intact. She had the feeling it was a friendly house, a happy house, the sort of house she would love to live in.

That's enough, she told herself firmly. It's not going to happen. It's over. This is the last job I'll do for Simon Delaware outside hospital. After that, he's on his own. He's got a housekeeper to run after him now.

The door opened. Mrs Rainer beamed with pleasure. 'Why, Dr Morgan, what a pleasant surprise! Do come in. I've just lit the fire in the sitting-room. Would you like some coffee?'

The sitting-room was warm and cosily inviting as Hannah sank down into one of the huge fireside armchairs. There was one each side of the crackling log fire—Obviously the place where the master and mistress of the house spent their evenings when the children were asleep upstairs.

Hannah looked into the fire and told herself to stop

109

being so sentimental. But all around her the oak
beams, the carefully cherished brass ornaments, the old
watercolours and oil paintings, everything conspired to
underline what might have been, if only. . .

'How do you take your coffee?' Mrs Rainer asked
as she bustled back in from the kitchen.

'Black,' Hannah said. 'This is a beautiful room.'

'Yes, isn't it?' Mrs Rainer said, handing over the
delicate china cup and saucer. 'My husband and I spent
many happy hours in here. I hope you will. . .'

She broke off in mid-sentence. 'I'm so sorry. I was
forgetting that you and Mr Delaware are just good
friends, and not. . . But you see, there was something
about the way you behaved towards each other when
you were here. I couldn't help hoping. . .'

'No, we're definitely just good friends,' Hannah put
in quickly, to save further embarassment. 'Simon has
a commitment, and that's really why I'm here—to
explain the situation to you.'

Mrs Rainer ran a hand over her carefully brushed
short grey hair. 'A commitment? What exactly do
you mean?'

'Before I explain, Mrs Rainer, I must ask you not
to breathe a word of what I'm going to say to anyone.
You see. . .'

And then, as briefly and as sensitively as she could,
Hannah explained about Simon's commitment to the
mother of his child and his promise to Adele. She tried
to be as objective in her explanation as she could, but
inevitably her emotions began to take over, especially
when Mrs Rainer kept interrupting with expressions
of sympathy.

'What an impossible situation, my dear,' Mrs Rainer

said when Hannah had finished. 'I can see now why it would be impossible for you and Mr Delaware to. . . Well, I mean. . .'

'As I said, we're just good friends,' Hannah put in quickly. 'And that's the way it will stay. Simon is delighted to be reunited with his son, even though it's only for a couple of months.'

The older woman smiled. 'I'm looking forward to taking care of the little boy. But what a dreadful situation for poor Mr Delaware. You must have been a great comfort to him. I could tell. . . There I go again! Let's be practical about the situation. Now, come upstairs and advise me about which room you think young Michael would like to sleep in. Probably the pink room where my daughter slept, next to the master bedroom, but we'll have to do something about the décor.'

There was a lump in Hannah's throat as she looked out of the deep-set dormer window of the pink room towards the river and agreed that it would be perfect for Michael. Wisps of ivy trailed outside over the top of the window and the morning mist was dispersing, giving her a better view of the garden where the trees were shedding their leaves on the grass to form a red and yellow carpet.

Mrs Rainer bustled about the little bedroom, moving ornaments and adjusting the angle of the pictures, before she joined Hannah at the window.

'There's quite a bit of work to be done in the garden. The old gardener who comes in has been ill for a few weeks. Does Mr Delaware enjoy gardening?'

'I really couldn't say,' Hannah said. 'I must be off. I've got an outpatient clinic early this afternoon. Thank you for the coffee.'

She turned at the door. Mrs Rainer was following her.

'Such a pity you have to go. I hope you'll come back as often as you can. Now, tell me, what do you think I should do about the décor in here? Too feminine for a little boy, I think, so. . .'

'I would wait till Michael and his daddy get here,' Hannah said hurriedly. 'They'll probably like to choose it themselves.'

'Yes, I'm sure you're right. Goodbye, Dr Morgan. Lovely to see you again, and don't worry about Mr Delaware's secret. It's safe with me.'

Hannah's feet didn't touch the ground for the next few days. Working in hospital, she didn't have time to worry about how she would feel when Simon got back. It was only at night, when she was trying to have a few hours' precious sleep, that her apprehensive longing took over. She would tell herself over and over again that she was going to be firm, but deep down she knew it would be a terrible struggle between her head and her heart.

The following Thursday Hannah found it difficult to concentrate as she started the afternoon clinic, knowing that Simon would be arriving at his house. She found herself wondering if Mrs Rainer had got everything ready for him. She began to think about the following day, when he would be back in hospital; she would be professional but decidedly cool with him. He had to understand that——

The door was opening. She'd asked Rona Phillips to send the first patient in.

'Oh God! Simon!' She clamped her hand over her

mouth. 'You startled me. I was expecting the first patient and. . .'

'You look as if you've seen a ghost. I told you I was coming back today.'

'Yes, but you're not due back in hospital until tomorrow.'

'Hannah, oh, Hannah.' He reached down to pull her to her feet from the chair.

The room was spinning round. She had to resist his strong arms. She held herself rigid but he pulled her against him, nuzzling his mouth against her hair, oblivious to her resistance. And then his mouth, his demanding mouth was on hers, and arrows of dormant passion were shooting down her spine, threatening to obliterate her well-thought-out strategies.

'Simon, we have to talk. We. . .'

'Later, Hannah; I hadn't realised how much I would miss you until. . .'

There was a discreet knocking on the door and then it was opening. Hannah wrenched herself away from Simon's embrace.

Rona Phillips came into the room, her eyes looking from one to the other.

'Shall I hold off the first patient?' she asked quietly.

'No!' Hannah said firmly, at the same time as Simon said, 'Yes, of course. There'll be a ten-minute delay while Dr Morgan brings me up to date. You'd better open up my consulting-room, Nurse Phillips. I'll see some of the patients on Dr Morgan's list.'

'Simon!' Hannah watched as the door closed behind the staff nurse. He was actually locking the door of her consulting-room. How dared he?

'No more interruptions,' he said softly, reaching out

to pull her into his arms. 'I've waited nearly three weeks for this moment. It's a pity it has to be in hospital. I hope you're free this evening because. . .'

'Simon, we need to talk!' she said desperately as his encircling arms began to undermine her determination. Oh, God! It was so good to feel him close to her again, the rasping touch of his stubbly cheek on hers, his mouth gently teasing until she opened hers and succumbed to his sensuous kiss.

'I can see you're tense because we're in your consulting-room,' he said gently, relinquishing his embrace. 'But tonight. . .'

'Tonight we'll talk, Simon,' she said firmly. 'I've been thinking while you were away.'

'Sounds ominous! What's the problem?'

She drew in her breath. 'The problem is our relationship; where it's going. As far as I can see——'

She broke off as she saw the worried expression appear on his face.

'Let's discuss it tonight,' he said quietly. 'Now, show me your patient list for the afternoon and we'll halve it together. You've been working too hard while I've been away. That's another reason why you're so tense and. . .'

'Where's Michael?' Hannah asked.

He straightened up from scrutinising the case-notes.

'He's at the house with Mrs Rainer. They're planning the décor of his bedroom. I've told him you're coming for supper and promised he can stay up to see you.'

She swallowed hard. The whole scenario was getting out of hand again. She was going to have to be as firm as she'd planned before Simon arrived back and threw her emotions into turmoil again.

'Let's get your first patient in,' Simon said, unlocking the door. 'I'll go across to my room and take your second. I've got the notes here. Staff Nurse Phillips can run between the two of us.'

Rona Phillips didn't utter a word when she brought the first patient in but her expression said it all. Hannah knew it would be all round the hospital by the end of the afternoon that Simon Delaware had returned from the States, gone immediately to see Hannah Morgan, even though he wasn't due back until tomorrow, and that it had taken them ten minutes to effect their reunion!

Her first patient was Valerie Simpson with baby Daniel.

'Sorry to keep you waiting, Valerie. Mr Delaware just got back from the States and we had things to discuss before I could start.'

She knew she was talking too quickly and she made an effort to slow down and concentrate on her patient. 'Now, let me have a look. How old is Daniel now? Nearly six months? He's in very good shape. How are you feeling Valerie?'

Valerie said she was feeling fine. It was all working out well at Colin's mum's house.

'She's a real mum to me,' Valerie said as she climbed on the examination couch. 'Spoils me rotten. . .and Daniel, too. She baths him, feeds him. He must think he's got two mums.'

Hannah nodded as she palpated Valerie's abdomen. 'Everything back in place here.' Her fingers went back over Valerie's uterus. There was a definite swelling; nothing too noticeable but she needed to check it out.

'Valerie, how are your periods?'

'Bit erratic, Doctor. I had one about three months ago. Haven't had one since I moved in with Colin.'

'And have you been using any form of contraception?'

'Oh, no! Colin would love another baby. So would his mum!'

'Maybe we should give you a pregnancy test, Valerie,' Hannah said.

Valerie gave a big smile. 'Really! Do you think I'm pregnant, Doctor?'

'Too early to say without a pregnancy test. So, I'd like you to pop along to the treatment-room and they'll test your urine. Come back to me when you've seen them.' Hannah filled in a form for Valerie. 'Give them this,' she said.

Rona Phillips brought in the next patient as soon as Valerie had gone off to the treatment-room.

Hannah smiled, glancing briefly at the notes as she asked her patient to sit down.

Catherine Benson was a good-looking woman of twenty-seven. Hannah remembered her as being a pleasant, easygoing, relaxed person; the sort of patient who made things easier for herself and the medical staff by being relaxed and co-operative.

'I remember you told me you were a nurse before you had your first baby, Mrs Benson. How does it feel to be on the receiving end of the treatment?'

The patient smiled, easing herself back against the chair and placing both hands over the large blue hand-knitted sweater that covered her rounded abdomen.

'It's great! I'm feeling very fit and I enjoy coming back into hospital to see all the latest technology. I used to work over at Leeds Infirmary as a staff nurse in ENT, so Obstetrics is a new field for me. Mike and I moved to Moortown when we were married and Tessa was born a year later. She's three now. We were thrilled when I knew I was expecting again but we hadn't expected twins!' Catherine Benson laughed. 'We haven't any twins in the family at all!'

'They're most likely to be identical, then,' Hannah said. 'One of your eggs divided and made two babies.'

Catherine Benson smiled and ran a hand through her short, curly fair hair. 'Double trouble! No, I don't mean that. Actually we're both delighted. It means I get the family I want in one fell swoop. We intend to call a halt at three. But there's just one thing, Dr Morgan. . .' Her voice trailed away and her eyes held a serious expression.

'Yes, go on, Catherine,' Hannah prompted gently. She had sensed ever since her patient came into the room that she had something on her mind, something that was worrying her behind her veneer of total acceptance of the situation.

'Well, just before I had Tessa, we found out she was going to be a breech presentation. My doctor tried to turn her around so her head would come out first, but he couldn't. So he said he wanted to do a Caesarean because it would be safer.'

The patient paused and Hannah glanced at the notes to refresh her memory.

'Yes, you were a patient of Mr Horace Dixon, weren't you?'

Catherine Benson nodded, a worried look stealing over her face. 'That's why I specially asked if I could be treated by the Delaware firm this time. One of my friends from our nursing days told me that Mr Dixon

favours Caesareans, whereas Mr Delaware prefers
natural births if possible. Is that true, Dr Morgan?'

Hannah paused. It certainly was true, but she
couldn't be so unprofessional as to admit it, even to
an ex-nurse. In fact, when she came to think about it,
especially not to an ex-nurse, who might repeat her
words verbatim to other colleagues. Better to be totally
impartial in this delicate situation. There was nothing
wrong with Horace Dixon's attitude but, like Simon,
she favoured natural birth unless they were expecting
exceptionally difficult complications.

'I'll tell you what I'll do, Catherine,' Hannah said,
completely avoiding answering the question about
Horace Dixon's methods. 'I'll put down your feelings
on the subject of Caesarean section in your notes.
When it's time to deliver your twins I'll try to be around
if I possibly can. Hopefully, there won't be any complications, but if there are. . .'

'It's not that I'm scared of a Caesarean,' the patient
interrupted. 'But I want to enjoy my twins right from
the start. I want to sit up in bed and feed them without
feeling the pull on my abdominal wound, and I want to
be totally aware of what's going on when they actually
arrive. Somehow, I felt I'd been cheated last time——'
She broke off. 'You don't think I'm being silly, do you
Doctor?'

Hannah leaned over and patted her patient's hand.
'Of course not. They're your precious babies and you
have a right to determine how you'd like them to be
born. Now, you've just had your scan, haven't you?
Let me have a look at the results, Catherine.'

'There didn't seem much room left in my abdomen
when I watched the screen,' the patient said, reverting

to her usual cheery self. 'They're both jostling against each other. Sometimes they wake me up in the night and it feels as if they're playing football together.'

Hannah smiled as she looked down the check-list. Everything appeared normal, but she would keep an especially watchful eye on this patient, in view of the fact that she was expecting twins and also that she was averse to having a Caesarean.

'Staff Nurse thinks they're both boys,' Mrs Benson said happily. 'She pointed out on the screen where they both had that essential extra bit, but I couldn't make it out myself.'

'Staff Nurse has written down here that she thinks they're boys,' Hannah said. 'Next time you're here I'll go in with you and check it out myself.'

'I don't mind what they are so long as they're healthy,' the patient said.

'Well, then, let me help you up on the couch and I'll examine you,' Hannah said.

At the end of the examination Hannah told her patient she was in very good condition, and on course for natural births for her twins.

'You're due at the beginning of January but it could be earlier; twins often are,' Hannah said.

'The sooner the better,' her patient said. 'They feel heavy enough already. 'Thanks, Doctor. I hope you'll be there at the birth.'

'I'll try my best,' Hannah assured her. Only the direst emergency in Theatre would stop her from being in on this case.

Rona Phillips brought her a cup of tea. She had a few sips and then called in the next patient. They were running behind schedule.

She smiled encouragingly at the nervous first-time mother-to-be as she began her examination.

When this patient went out, Valerie Simpson came charging through the door on her return from the treatment-room. She was smiling all over her face.

'Positive!' she said, handing a form to Hannah.

'Congratulations!' Hannah said. 'We'll ask Staff Nurse to take you down to ultrasound for a scan. You can leave Daniel with me.'

After Valerie had gone she put baby Daniel in the cot beside her desk, talking to him as she lowered him in.

'Who's a good little boy, then?'

Daniel gurgled and laughed up at her.

There was a discreet cough from the direction of the doorway.

'I hadn't realised we were running a creche,' Simon said with a smile.

'It's baby Daniel—Valerie Simpson's baby. The one you delivered at the roadside after the car crash.'

Simon's eyes were tender as he looked into the cot. 'He looks very healthy. Why are you looking after him?'

'I've just sent Valerie off to ultrasound for a scan. She's pregnant again.'

'How does she feel about it?'

'She's ecstatic. Did you want something, Simon?'

'Yes, I need some information about Pamela Bewley, the patient we induced because of pre-eclampsia back in May. Have you got the case-notes of that delivery? There isn't enough information on the computer.'

Hannah riffled through her pile of notes and came up with the relevant document.

Their hands touched as she handed it over. Simon looked pointedly at his watch. 'Can you meet me in the car park at six?' he said quietly.

'It will be a rush, but I expect I can make it.'

She turned away, looking for the notes on the next patient.

'There's something wrong, isn't there?' he said evenly.

She looked up. 'Yes, I've been thinking while you were away and. . . Look, I can't explain here, in the middle of the clinic.'

'Tonight, then,' he said gently. 'We'll sort out what's worrying you together.'

She took a deep breath to steady her nerves after he'd gone. It had all seemed so much simpler when he was three thousand miles away. But now that he was here in the flesh, now that she'd allowed him to kiss her, to hold her in his arms. . .

'The notes for the late arrival patient are here,' Staff Nurse Phillips said, coming in briskly. 'Her GP phoned to see if we would fit her in today.'

'Bring her in,' Hannah said, glancing at the notes, which told her that Judith Brown, age twenty-four, had been examined by her GP who suspected she might have an ovarian cyst.

'Come in and sit down over here, Mrs Brown. Let's have a little chat before I examine you.'

Hannah could see, instantly, that her patient was extremely worried. She was a small, thin woman, with fair wispy hair and a pale complexion, and her fingers were knotting and unknotting as she talked.

'My doctor told me he thinks I've got an ovarian cyst. Is that a growth, Doctor?' Mrs Brown asked.

'If you do have an ovarian cyst, Mrs Brown, I would describe it as an abnormal fluid-filled swelling in one of the ovaries.'

'I'm not too sure what ovaries do. Could you explain them to me?'

'Your ovaries are the little glands on either side of the uterus, just below the entrance to the Fallopian tubes. The ovaries release the eggs that grow into babies if they're fertilised. Most women will probably have had at least one ovarian cyst without knowing it. They can appear at any age, in any number, and on one or both ovaries. They often disappear on their own without any treatment.'

'Do you think mine will disappear?'

'I can't say until I've had a look. I'll examine you and see if that's what you've got, and then we'll decide what to do, Mrs Brown. Now, if you'd just like to get up on this couch. . .'

Hannah was mentally reviewing the symptoms her patient had described during their talk. Judith Brown had said she found intercourse painful, her periods were heavy and irregular, she had to pass water frequently and recently she'd felt nauseous and had suffered bouts of abdominal pain. Hannah had taken her temperature and discovered it was too high—not dangerously so, but indicating an abnormality.

She pulled on a pair of surgical gloves and did an internal examination. Her patient was very tense and it wasn't easy to get her to relax. At the end of her examination Hannah decided it would be necessary to perform a laparoscopy, and the sooner the better.

She sat down beside the couch and explained what she was going to do.

'I'd like to admit you today, Mrs Brown, so we can have a better look at what's going on. Will that cause problems back at your home?'

'No, my husband can look after himself. We haven't got any family. We've been trying ever since we got married four years ago but we're still on our own. That's one reason I went to my doctor in the first place. What are you going to do with me, Doctor?'

'Tomorrow we'll take you down to Theatre, give you a general anaesthetic, and then do a minor operation called a laparoscopy. That means we can look into your abdomen through a sort of viewing-tube. Now, if we do find you have an ovarian cyst, we'll remove it.'

'Is that because you think it might be cancer?'

'No, it's not,' Hannah said quickly. 'Most ovarian cysts are benign—that means they don't cause any more problems.'

'But if it wasn't benign. . . What's the other kind— malignant isn't it? How can you tell the difference?'

'During the operation, a small piece of the cyst will be sent to the laboratory. There it will be quickly examined to find out whether it's benign or malignant. If it's benign, only the cyst will be removed, leaving the ovary in place. If it should be malignant then we would remove the cyst, the ovary and the Fallopian tube. But we're rushing ahead, Mrs Brown. Let's go one step at a time.'

Hannah watched her patient's reaction. She knew she'd been worried when she first arrived, but after her explanation Mrs Brown seemed more relaxed. She'd found it was always best to explain everything to her patients. If they confronted the worst thing that could happen to them, then they were more likely to settle down and accept the outcome. And in the majority of cases there was no cause for alarm.

'Don't worry, Mrs Brown,' Hannah said gently as her patient got off the examination couch. 'If we look at the statistics, this cyst is much more likely to be benign than malignant.'

Her patient smiled. 'Thanks, Doctor. I like to be told what's going on. It helps if you get treated like a person rather than a case-number. Will you call me Judith, please? That helps, too—more friendly, isn't it?'

Hannah smiled back. 'Some patients prefer not to know what's going on. I never force information on those. But if patients ask questions I always answer truthfully, so fire away, Judith.'

Hannah spent a few more minutes answering her patient's questions before making a phone call through to Nightingale to ask Sister Gregson to admit her patient to the gynaecological unit and prepare her for Theatre in the morning.

At the end of the afternoon she had only ten minutes to get ready. Flinging off her white coat, she pulled on a stone-coloured sweater and matching woollen trousers. She was surprised to find how nervous she was. The source of the nerves, she decided, was as much at meeting Simon's young son, Michael, as at telling Simon she'd decided not to see him any more outside hospital.

At six o'clock she hurried into the car park. He was there already, pushing open his passenger door as she arrived. The car's engine sprang to life. She sat very still, trying to get rid of her tense feelings, and they drove out of the car park, turning into the rush-hour traffic.

Once clear of the town she began to relax. It was going to be OK. All she had to do was remember that there was no future in her relationship with Simon. This was positively the last time she would be alone with him.

But, turning sideways, she looked at Simon's handsome profile, his thick dark hair, his sensitive surgeon's hands gripping the wheel, and her heart gave its customary hop, skip and a jump. With a jolt she realised she loved this man—for better for worse. . .

Well, that was an unfortunate phrase to think of, she told herself—for better for worse. Would she go on and quote the phrase 'for richer for poorer'? Her heart started beating rapidly as she remembered the phrases from all the weddings she'd been to in the past.

On all those occasions she'd wondered how anybody could make such a huge commitment, give themselves up to another person. But she was beginning to realise now that if you loved someone enough then there wouldn't be a problem. . .would there. . .?

'You're very quiet.'

'I was thinking about that suspected ovarian cyst I admitted,' she improvised quickly. 'It's going to be a very long list tomorrow, but I don't want to delay Judith Brown's laparoscopy.'

'We can easily cope with the extra work tomorrow. We'll put Mrs Brown first on the list,' he said. 'Now, stop talking shop. What's really worrying you?'

She took a deep breath. 'I don't know if I can go along like this, Simon.'

'Neither do I,' he said quietly.

She glanced up at him to see a serious expression clouding his face. He looked grim, determined and tense as he negotiated the winding road down into Cragdale. She didn't want to add to his worries but she had to say something before they went any further. She couldn't leave it until they found an opportunity to be alone in the house.

'While you were away I had time to think,' she began tentatively. 'And I decided that I couldn't go on waiting around for you in a supposedly platonic relationship. I've got my own life to lead. I can't take a half-life with you. You're not free, and. . .'

'No, I'm not free,' he interrupted harshly. 'You don't need to remind me. I never will be free while Felicity's body is linked up to that infernal machine. . . Oh, God, I shouldn't have said that. . .'

Hannah watched the whitening of his knuckles as he gripped the wheel, steering the car across the bridge to approach the house.

'Yes, you should have said it,' she said gently. 'You can't go on pretending to be a saint, waiting around for someone to sanction the ending of a life that actually ended more than five years ago.'

He switched off the engine at the end of the drive in front of the house and turned towards her, reaching out for her hands. She felt the strong grasp of his fingers and her legs turned to jelly. He only had to look at her in that tender, intimate way that she'd come to love and she was a goner. It was hopeless; she couldn't leave him. However long it took, she knew she would want to wait. But supposing it went on for years. . .

He leaned forward and kissed her gently on the lips. As he pulled away he looked into her eyes with the sort of expression that would have melted away the most determined resolutions.

'Thank you for saying that. It's good to know you don't condemn my occasional outbursts against the system that keeps Felicity's body alive.'

'You have to release your tension somehow. It's not good to go bottling it up all the time. I don't mind if you use me as a sounding-board. . .'

She broke off, knowing that she was reaffirming her commitment to him.

He took one of her hands, turning it palm-upwards and gently placing it against his lips.

'I do need ways of releasing tension, but there are better ways than losing my temper,' he said quietly, his eyes intently watching her reaction.

'Are you propositioning me, Mr Delaware?' she asked, with pseudo-coyness.

He laughed. 'Not at this particular moment, Dr Morgan. But perhaps we could get together later. . .'

'I came out here tonight to tell you I wouldn't see you again outside hospital, but. . .' She stopped and gave a sigh of exasperation.

'I hope I can get you to change your mind,' he said, pulling her against him roughly as his lips claimed hers again.

As the kiss ended he spoke tenderly, his lips almost touching hers. 'I'm not free in the technical sense, but I'm not a monk in a monastery, bound to a vow of chastity. I need you, Hannah. I want to make love to you. . .'

'Daddy!'

The childish cry startled Hannah. She pulled away from Simon's embrace, trying to quell the emotional turmoil and sensual excitement he'd aroused inside her. She could see a small boy running out of the brass-studded oak door.

'Michael!'

Simon had leapt out of the car and was running towards his son.

She took a deep breath as she pulled open the passenger door and went along to join them, all the time mulling over what she should do.

What could she do? She ought to cut and run, but she was hopelessly in love with this man, and the thought of a physical relationship was sending her wild with desire. . .

CHAPTER EIGHT

HANNAH was decidedly nervous as she watched the reunion of father and son. Simon had lifted Michael up into his arms so that the child's face was level with her own. She thought how much he looked like Simon, and immediately her heart went out to him. His eyes were the same dark brown, the cheekbones firm and aristocratic, and she noticed the small cleft in his chin. Yes, this was unmistakably Simon's son. His eyes held a wary expression, she noticed, as if he was sizing her up, wondering what sort of grown-up she was going to turn out to be, and possibly worrying that she might want to take up too much of his daddy's time.

'Hello, Michael, I'm Hannah,' she said, holding out her hand.

The boy hesitated before putting out his own hand to grasp hers in a politely formal handshake.

'I'm Michael. You work with Daddy don't you? Do you help him cut people up?'

Hannah remained solemn, but she could see Simon was having a hard time trying not to laugh.

'Yes, Michael, we both work in the operating-theatres doing surgical operations. Then, when we've put things right, we take the patients back to the ward and take care of them there.'

'Who's looking after your patients while you're here having supper?' the little boy asked, a worried expression spreading across his face.

Hannah found Michael's Boston accent enchanting. It was more pronounced than his father's, no doubt because he'd been born there—unlike Simon, who'd been born in England to English parents, she remembered. She smiled as she listened to Simon explaining that there was a team of doctors and nurses to take care of the patients while they were away.

'In fact, we could stay out all night if we wanted to,' he finished off, his eyes watching Hannah's reaction.

She felt the quickening of her pulse. What would she do if Simon asked her to stay? The thought of lying in his arms all night was too ecstatic to contemplate, but. . .

'Did you bring your toothbrush?' The little boy's voice interrupted her thoughts.

'No, I didn't.' She looked up at Simon, who was giving her a rakish grin.

'Not an insurmountable problem,' he said evenly. 'Shall we go inside? It's getting chilly out here.'

She felt Simon's arm briefly encircle her waist as they went in and tried desperately to get a grip on her emotions.

'Dr Morgan, how lovely to see you again.' Mrs Rainer, the friendly housekeeper was coming down the hall with her hand outstretched in welcome. 'And you've met Michael. I couldn't keep him inside any longer. As soon as he heard your car drive through the gates he wanted to rush out, but I told him he must give Daddy and his guest a couple of minutes to catch their breath.'

Mrs Rainer was deliberately avoiding eye contact, but Hannah knew that she must have looked out of the window, must have seen their most unprofessional kiss. But then, right from the start she'd had them marked out as lovers. But they weren't. . .not yet.

Hannah gave an involuntary shiver.

'You're cold, my dear,' Mrs Rainer said. 'Come into the sitting-room and get warm. These October nights can be very chilly.'

Simon went into the kitchen and emerged seconds later with a tray of glasses and an ice-bucket containing a bottle of champagne. Michael followed behind him, carefully carrying a small glass of orange juice.

'Will you have a glass of champagne with us, Mrs Rainer?' Simon asked.

'No, thank you; it goes straight to my head and puts me off my cooking. Besides, I'm not part of the celebration—whatever it is.'

'We're not celebrating,' Simon said. 'Just saying that this is the first day of the rest of our lives.'

Hannah could feel a blush threatening to envelop her face.

Mrs Rainer was smiling as she went back to the kitchen, from where wonderful cooking smells were wafting.

Simon popped the cork and poured out the champagne.

'Cheers!' he said, and Michael echoed him as the three of them clinked their glasses together.

'I gather you've decided not to drive out again tonight,' Hannah said, watching Simon drain his glass and pour out another one. 'I presume there's a taxi service in the village to get me back to hospital.'

He put out his hand and took hold of hers. 'Let's cross that bridge when we come to it.'

The pressure of his fingers unnerved her. How could

she hold out against this man. . .or indeed against her own treacherous emotions? But then why should she hold out? Why not swim along with the tide? Allow herself one night of madness before. . .before the rest of her life, as Simon had so aptly put it.

'Supper's ready.' Mrs Rainer came in, wiping her damp hands on the frilly apron that covered her navy blue woollen dress with its white Peter Pan collar.

The dining-room table was set for three.

'I'd rather eat in the kitchen,' Mrs Rainer explained. 'I can keep an eye on things without having to keep jumping up and down. Michael can eat in there with me if he likes. . .'

'Oh, no,' Hannah said. 'We'd prefer to have him with us, wouldn't we, Simon?'

'Can I sit between you and Daddy?' Michael asked, tugging at Hannah's hand.

'Yes, of course.' Hannah lifted the little boy on to the chair at the head of the table. 'I think we're going to need a cushion, Simon. . .'

Simon's eyes were tender as he brought her the cushion and put it underneath his son.

'I think you two are going to be great friends,' he said softly.

Hannah felt a lump rising in her throat. This charming little boy was easing his way into her affections just as his father had done.

Mrs Rainer produced home-made vegetable soup, rack of lamb with mint sauce, roast potatoes and cauliflower cheese. It became evident towards the end of the main course that Michael wasn't hungry and was falling asleep.

'I gave Michael some supper before you arrived,'

Mrs Rainer said, bustling in to collect the plates. 'But then he told me you'd promised he could stay up to spend some time with you.'

'I'll take him up to bed,' Simon said, picking up the almost sleeping boy.

Michael's head lolled against Simon's shirt and he stopped trying to stay awake as he was carried out through the door.

Hannah helped Mrs Rainer to clear the table and bring in the fruit, cheese and coffee. Simon returned as Hannah was pouring out three cups, Mrs Rainer having said she would join them for a few minutes.

'I have to go over to my sister's tonight, over in Beckdale. She's not been well and I promised to go if I could. I didn't know you would be here today, Mr Delaware, when I arranged to go. I would have cancelled if you'd wanted me to babysit, but when you said you didn't have to go back to the hospital tonight I thought, well——'

She broke off and Hannah thought how evasive she sounded. There was no doubt in Hannah's mind that the older woman was clearing off so that they could be alone.

'Anyway, don't worry about me,' Dorothy Rainer continued. 'I've got my little car and it's only five miles over the next hill. I'll be back first thing in the morning to make breakfast and look after Michael. What time will you need to leave, Mr Delaware?'

'Let me see, I've got to be in Theatre at nine, but I need to see a few patients first. I'd better be off by seven-thirty, Mrs Rainer.'

'I'll make breakfast for seven o'clock. . . Goodnight.'

They were alone. Hannah suddenly felt uncharacteristically shy.

Simon reached across the table and took hold of her hand. 'Don't look so worried. I'll call you a taxi if you really want to go back.'

She faced him, her eyes wide with anticipation, her body smouldering with an intense need to be close to him.

'That's the trouble. I don't want to go back, I want to stay. . . But Simon, it's madness, it's. . .'

'It's time we injected a bit of madness into our lives.' He rounded the table and grasped both her hands, pulling her to her feet so that he could hold her in his arms.

She sighed as she leaned against his chest, aware of the beating of his heart through the thin cotton shirt. She could smell the faint scent of his aftershave. She'd noticed it before, but now it was adding to the excitement she felt, stimulating the sensual arousal deep inside her. Yes, she wanted Simon to make love to her tonight, and she'd think about the consequences afterwards.

She heard Mrs Rainer walking down the hall, calling out, 'Goodnight.'

The front door closed; seconds later there was the sound of a car driving off.

She looked up into Simon's eyes and saw her own excitement mirrored there.

'Let's go to bed,' he whispered, drawing her against his side.

Hannah realised she was trembling as they climbed the staircase to the first floor. She took a deep breath as Simon opened the door to the master bedroom.

He led her inside. The red damask curtains of the four-poster bed were drawn back. The counterpane was in the same material as the curtains and Simon removed it to reveal white linen sheets. He turned and held out his hands towards her.

It was like being in a dream in slow motion as she crossed the room and went into his arms. But the pace quickened as they came close and began to undress each other. Hannah sensed they had both been holding out for far too long. When their naked skin touched, she gave an involuntary sigh.

And then Simon was lifting her on to the bed, his hands caressing her, exciting her with the touch of his sensitive fingers. She stopped thinking about the consequences, about the future, about what would happen if. . . Because there was only the present. This mad, sensuous, exciting present. And as their bodies fused together Hannah let out an ecstatic cry at the joy of fulfilment.

'Oh, Simon,' she whispered afterwards as she snuggled against him, wondering how long it would be before she had to come down from cloud nine. Her whole body tingled with consummated passion and she knew life could never be the same again. This man had started a fire that wouldn't easily be put out, but she would think about that later—much later.

He kissed her gently, ever so gently, then his lips hardened, his tongue became more demanding as their mouths blended together in a deeply satisfying lovers' kiss.

And then he was pulling away from her, swinging his legs over the side of the bed. She watched him cross the room to where a half unpacked suitcase stood on the window-seat. She remembered that it was only today he'd arrived back from the States. He pulled a white towelling bathrobe from inside. Knotting the belt, he returned to the bed, sitting down beside her to stroke her hair.

'I've wanted to make love to you for so long,' he said huskily. 'But I felt I had no right to ask you because. . .'

'Because you're not free,' she said evenly, her spirits plummeting as the reality of the situation forced itself upon her again. She hauled herself up against the pillows, pulling the sheet against her naked skin. 'You don't need to remind me again that if you don't stay free for Felicity Adele will keep Michael.'

He moved round to the other side of the bed, propping himself against his pillows. Their heads were only inches away from each other as Simon took hold of Hannah's hand.

'Please let me explain once more,' he said. 'When I was in the States, I decided I had to go and see Felicity again, to make sure that in my own mind I hadn't exaggerated her condition over the last five years. One of the nurses took me into her room. I looked down at the motionless patient in the bed, wired up to the life-support machine, and realised I hadn't exaggerated. It was the empty shell of a woman with whom I'd had a brief affair over five years ago. The affair had finished months before she crashed her car and went into a permanent coma. . .'

Hannah held her breath as he paused. Had he finally found a way to set himself free from this intolerable situation?

'But at the same time,' he continued solemnly, 'I

still have a duty towards her. I can't abandon her.
She's still the mother of my son. And I have to keep
my promise to Adele.'

'But Felicity's been brain dead for over five years.
If she was one of our patients you would be urging
her relatives to switch off the support system, wouldn't
you?' Hannah said quietly.

He turned tormented eyes towards her. 'But she's
not one of my patients. She's the mother of my son.
I can't be free until her death certificate has been
signed. But that doesn't mean I don't love you,
Hannah. It doesn't mean we can't make love. But the
guilt that comes over me when I think. . .'

'Stop tormenting yourself, Simon!' Hannah threw
back the sheets as she reached for her clothes, her
back towards him as she dragged them on. 'We knew
it was madness to become too heavily involved with
each other. If you're stricken with guilt by what we've
done, then we'd better not see each other again outside
hospital.'

'Hannah, I couldn't bear to lose you,' Simon said,
his arms reaching out and hauling her, semi-clothed,
back on to the bed. 'I love you desperately.'

She closed her eyes, feeling his hot kisses raining on
her face. 'And I love you, Simon,' she whispered,
feeling her treacherous body reacting once more to his
passion. There was no solution to their situation, but
the inevitable fire that sprang up between them
couldn't be put out.

This time their lovemaking was gentler, more con-
trolled, more meaningful: the lovemaking of two
people who'd explored each other's bodies before and
knew exactly how to reach the heights of ecstasy.

Afterwards Hannah curled up against Simon, and fell into a deep, undisturbed, dreamless sleep.

She awoke to the shrilling of an alarm clock. As she listened to the sound it gradually dawned on her that it wasn't hers. The sound stopped. Someone had switched it off. She opened her eyes and reality flooded back.

Simon was lying on his back, staring at the top of the four-poster bed. The tormented expression that she'd seen the night before when he described his visit to Felicity was back. She could see he was racked with guilt and there wasn't a thing she could do about it. Human emotions were unpredictably difficult to understand. She asked herself how she would feel if she were in the same situation as Simon, and decided that she would probably feel exactly the same. Because, in a strange way, some of the guilt he was feeling had rubbed off on her. She felt she didn't have the right to take this man away from the mother of his child, lying utterly defenceless and helpless in that hospital bed three thousand miles away. . .

Simon rolled on to his side and kissed her gently. She allowed herself a quick response before jumping out of bed.

'I'm going to take a taxi,' she said quickly. 'I'll escape before Mrs Rainer gets back.'

She turned briefly at the bathroom door, and thought she saw relief on his face. As she went into the bathroom and ran herself a bath she thought that the reality of their night of passion was becoming sleazy. She'd been a one-night stand with a man who wasn't free. The fact that she was desperately in love with this man didn't seem to make much difference in the cold light of day.

When she emerged, Simon was fully clothed. He handed her a cup of strong coffee.

'I've ordered you a taxi. He'll be here in a few minutes. I decided to call one out from Moortown.'

She took a sip of the coffee. 'So that the local cabby doesn't spread gossip all over the village?' she said lightly.

'I don't even know if there is a cabby in the village,' he said defensively.

'Anyway, thanks for saving my reputation,' she said, putting on the jacket that Simon had retrieved from downstairs while she'd been in the bath.

She heard the sound of an engine in the drive.

'Goodbye.' She didn't even stop for a goodbye kiss. There had been too many kisses. . .but she wasn't sorry. Guilty, perhaps, but not sorry.

She was back in hospital just after seven and went along to the canteen for some toast and coffee. A group of nurses were surrounding one table, a couple of doctors were at another, otherwise the place was deserted.

She tensed as she saw Sara coming in, looking decidedly weary after her night in charge of Nightingale. She was followed by James Dewhirst, one of the housemen.

'It's all right for some,' Sara said, joining Hannah at her table. 'James and I have been rushed off our feet all night.'

'You'd better get some sleep,' Hannah said, standing up. 'I'm just on my way to Nightingale, then I'll be in Theatre.'

'I came to your room to see if you wanted a coffee last night but you weren't in,' Sara said. 'Go anywhere nice?'

'Saw my parents,' Hannah said. The lie came out without a second's thought and she hated the feeling that followed it. She was becoming devious, guilt-ridden, and all because she'd fallen for the wrong man.

As she went along the corridor that led to Nightingale she wondered just how long she could keep up the pretence that there was nothing between Simon and herself. Was it worth it? Wouldn't it be better to end a relationship that had no foreseeable future?

When Simon walked into Theatre at nine Hannah could see that he too was struggling to conceal his feelings. He barely glanced at her across the table, merely putting out his gloved hand to indicate that he wanted a scalpel for the first incision.

This is how it will be, Hannah thought as she watched Simon's fingers trace the short line across the patient's abdomen. A night of illicit passion followed by a guilt-ridden day trying to remain professional, trying to cover up our feelings for each other.

As Simon began to explain what was happening to the students, in his professional teaching voice, she gave herself a mental shake and brought all her attention on to the operation in progress.

'Our patient, Judith Brown, is aged twenty-four; her GP referred her to us yesterday and we decided to admit her. The signs are that she may have an ovarian cyst, which is an abnormal growth on the ovaries, the egg-producing organs in the female body. Now that

I've made a small incision through the abdominal wall I'm going to take a look at the left ovary through this viewing-tube. . . And, yes, there is a small cyst. I'm going to cut out a piece of the cyst which we'll have examined in the lab before we go any further.'

During the minutes when the cyst was being examined Simon continued to teach the students, answering their questions on the operation in hand and the ones to come later on the list. Hannah found herself marvelling at the way he could put on this extrovert act of successful surgeon, not a care in the world, when inside, she knew, he was racked with emotional turmoil.

A lab technician brought back the small piece of ovarian cyst with the good news that it was benign, or harmless.

Simon gave a relieved smile. 'Good! All we need to do now is remove the cyst and leave the ovary in place. I'll check the other ovary.'

The other ovary proved to be perfectly healthy. Hannah sutured the abdomen while Simon went to check on the next patient waiting to be anaesthetised in the ante-room.

At the end of the list Hannah went along to Nightingale, to check on her post-operative patients. She found Judith Brown fully round from her anaesthetic and gave her the good news that the cyst was harmless.

Mrs Brown smiled. 'Thank goodness! Did you have to take away the ovary?'

'No, it's still in place and looking very healthy.'

'I'm glad about that because we're still hoping for a family, and I suppose two ovaries are better than one when you're hoping to produce the precious eggs that are potential babies.'

'You might find that you'll conceive more easily now that the cyst has been removed. That could well have been the cause of your infertility. Have you and your husband had all the other infertility checks?'

The patient nodded. 'Everything else is OK.'

Hannah smiled. 'Well, good luck, then!'

Mrs Brown smiled back. 'How soon can I go home?'

Hannah heard the firm tread of footsteps across the ward floor and knew, instinctively, that it was Simon. She turned to look at him.

'Mrs Brown can't wait to get home so she can start her family,' she said. 'When shall we let her escape, Mr Delaware?'

Simon gave the patient one of his charming smiles and patted her hand. 'Can you contain yourself for a couple of days, Mrs Brown?'

Hannah saw the look of admiration on their patient's face. He can still charm the birds from the trees, she thought, even though he's suffering inside.

'I'll try,' Judith Brown said. 'And thank you, Mr Delaware. It must be wonderful to be a surgeon and solve people's problems.'

'It is,' Simon said evenly.

He looked across the bed at Hannah, and as their eyes met she saw the deep sadness behind the outer veneer. Simon could solve other people's problems but not his own.

CHAPTER NINE

FOR the next couple of months Hannah continued to work side by side with Simon in hospital, but neither of them made any moves to see each other outside. Hannah had resigned herself to the fact that the night they'd spent together mustn't be repeated, and that to avoid this happening again she mustn't be alone with Simon. She sensed, also, that he'd suffered the pangs of guilt much more than she had.

Her off-duty time was spent shopping in Moortown, going for walks over the moors, or visiting her parents.

During the course of several visits, her mother had only made one reference to Simon, and that was to say that she was glad Hannah wasn't seeing 'that married doctor' any more. Hannah had insisted that Simon wasn't married, that there were other complications she wasn't free to disclose, but her mother had remained tight-lipped and unconvinced.

In hospital she put herself into her most professional mood whenever she was working with Simon, deliberately avoiding eye contact, being extremely polite, but trying to distance herself. Simon responded in the same vein and Hannah was sure that no one suspected they'd been lovers. Certainly the hospital grapevine seemed to have exhausted that line of enquiry, as far as she could tell.

But other rumours concerning Simon began to be bandied about. She first heard them when she was having coffee with Sister Gregson one morning, early in December.

'I've just been told that our Mr Delaware has a young son,' Sister Gregson said quietly. 'He's a dark horse, isn't he? I didn't even know he was married. Ruth Carson, one of my staff nurses, lives over at Cragdale, and her little boy, Richard, goes to the primary school there. She told me her son came home saying there was a new boy in his class called Michael Delaware. Then one day she saw Mr Delaware picking him up from the school, so it must be his boy. He's got a house in the village, apparently, but Mrs Delaware doesn't seem to be around. It's very strange, isn't it? Do you think. . .?'

'Sister, I've just remembered I have to check on a patient in Casualty, so if you'll excuse me. . .'

More lies, she thought as she hurried down the corridor, but she wasn't going to wait around listening to Sister's gossip. Speculation about Simon's private life would be all over the hospital before long. She supposed it had been inevitable since he'd brought Michael to live with him. The two months must be nearly up. He would have to go back to the States soon. She wondered how. . .

Rounding the corridor, she almost collided with Simon. For a moment they stood almost touching each other, only inches apart.

He gave her a slow, enigmatic smile. 'Steady on, why the rush?'

'I was escaping from Sister Gregson.' She hesitated. 'She isn't usually prone to gossip but she just told me that one of her nurses has a son at the same school as Michael. She's wondering why nobody knew you were married and so on. I thought I'd better tell you so that you can have your answers ready when the news leaks out.'

He gave a deep sigh of resignation. 'I suppose it was inevitable once Michael had started school.'

'So how will you explain about his mother?'

He frowned. 'I don't have to explain anything. I'm not on trial here. I shall simply decline to comment or answer any questions on the subject, as I've always done.'

He glanced around to see that no one was listening. A couple of nurses went past, their eyes drawn towards the two doctors, and a family of patient's relatives approached, intent on reaching the correct ward.

'Excuse me, Doctor, can you tell me the way to Male Surgical?' the mother asked.

Simon patiently explained, but he put out his hand to detain Hannah, who thought this might be a good time to escape. Just standing here in the corridor with Simon was undermining all the determination she'd had to use during the last couple of months.

The family were thanking Simon and hurrying away. He lowered his voice as he turned to speak to her. 'We can't talk here. Come back to my room. . .no strings attached,' he added, with a wry smile.

She nodded, trying to quell the surge of excitement that coursed through her treacherous body as they walked together towards the residents' quarters.

Memories flooded back as Simon unlocked the door and she followed him inside. It seemed so long ago, that night, almost seven months ago, when she'd had coffee and Michael had called on the phone.

'Come and sit down. Coffee?'

'No, thanks; I just had some with Sister Gregson.'

He joined her on the sofa. 'I'm glad you told me that the news about Michael is out.' He ran a hand through his thick dark hair. 'It's ironic, isn't it? I'm so proud of my son; I'd like to tell everybody how wonderful he is, but I have to keep quiet because Adele doesn't want Felicity's story to come out. When I was over there a couple of months ago, she told me she couldn't bear it if the Press got wind of the fact that she was refusing to switch off her daughter's life-support system.'

'How have you explained the situation to Michael?' Hannah asked gently.

She watched him as he got up and paced around the room.

'When Michael was small we told him that his mother was in hospital, but that she was too ill to see him. Adele looks after him like a mother and he rarely asks about his real mother.'

'So he's never seen Felicity?'

Simon shuddered. 'I couldn't allow him to see Felicity in the condition she's in. As it is, she's some mythical figure in his imagination. He has a photograph of her in his bedroom, taken during her acting career, when she was very beautiful. That's how he thinks of her.'

He paused. 'I'm glad I met you this morning. I've been wanting to ask you if. . .' He hesitated. 'Well, I have to take Michael back to the States for Christmas. Not long now. He's been asking when I'm going to bring the nice lady to see him again, and I wondered if you'd come over for supper. We've both decided to cool it, I know,' he hurried on, 'but it would make Michael so happy to see you.'

He was standing close to the sofa now. She looked up at him.

'Is that what I've become. . .the "nice lady" in your life?'

'Oh, Hannah!'

He pulled her to her feet, his arms encircling her in a tight embrace. 'You must know how much you mean to me, but——' He broke off in mid-sentence and closed his eyes, as if remembering.

'When I came back from the States I told myself that I couldn't let our relationship drift on in the same self-imposed, platonic way. I convinced myself that I had a right to a life of my own, that if news of an affair with you didn't reach Adele then it wouldn't matter. She would think I was keeping my promise. . .'

He drew in his breath. 'But I hadn't reckoned on what being with you would do to me. . .morally, physically, emotionally. . . Even if Adele didn't discover I'd broken my promise, I still had my own conscience to deal with. I would know that I hadn't kept my word. But in spite of that. . .'

He opened tormented eyes.

She held her breath as their eyes met, knowing that they were both fighting the desire to go further.

But the self-imposed dam had burst. Simon's mouth claimed hers and she gave herself up to the inevitable, to the ecstatic feeling of precious reunion with the man she couldn't stop loving, however hard she tried.

He pulled away, his eyes searching her face for signs of her reaction.

'My God, I've missed you so much!' he whispered

hoarsely. 'I've worked alongside you, touched your hand in the operating-theatre, stood oh, so close when we were putting up an IV. . . All the professional minutiae of hospital life, yet I knew I mustn't ever make love to you again, so I shouldn't even touch you or I'd set myself on fire. . . But I promise you, Hannah, if you come to supper I won't try to persuade you to stay the night. It. . .'

'If you remember, I didn't need persuading,' she said quietly. 'It was what we both wanted. . .a night of madness.'

'This time we'll just have supper,' he said, in a resigned, level voice.

'I'll drive out in my own car so I don't need a cab,' she said with a wry grin. 'If that's the end of the consultation, Mr Delaware, I think we should resume our professional lives.'

He gave her a slow, sad smile. 'My head tells me you're right, Dr Morgan.'

'So, let's go,' she said briskly, before her treacherous heart made her change her mind.

The following Wednesday Hannah drove her ancient Ford Fiesta out to Cragdale. She'd had a particularly busy day, but she'd noticed that Simon had restricted his outpatient appointments to the morning, saying that he had to leave hospital in the middle of the afternoon.

He came out of the house to meet her as she parked in his drive. He was looking relaxed in a hand-knitted, thick, chunky navy blue fisherman's sweater, worn over a plaid shirt and jeans. He opened her car door and held out his hand.

Their fingers touched and she swallowed hard. Got

to keep a clear head, she warned herself. Don't get emotional.

'So what was so important that you needed to go off so early?' she asked breezily, trying to get a grip on herself.

'I wanted to watch the rehearsal for Michael's nativity play. I can't make it tomorrow for the performance—I've been summoned to a meeting of the Board of Governors—so I asked the headmistress if I could go along this afternoon. So you see, it really was an important engagement.'

'How did it go—the rehearsal, I mean?'

She swung into step beside him, guiltily enjoying the feel of his hand on the back of her waist.

'You'd better ask Michael,' he said as the little boy rushed out through the door.

Hannah crouched down so as to be on a level with him, and he flung himself against her. She caught him in her arms, reassured by his friendly attitude towards her.

'I'm glad you've come, Hannah. I kept asking Daddy when you were coming again, but he said you were always too busy at the hospital. Do you work harder than Daddy?'

Hannah's eyes met Simon's, and they both laughed.

'Of course,' Hannah said. 'I'm not an important consultant like your daddy. I can't go home in the middle of the afternoon to watch nativity plays. What part do you play, Michael?'

'I'm the inn-keeper,' he said proudly. 'I have to say, "I'm sorry, we're full up," when Joseph asks if I have a room. But we were only practising today. Tomorrow is the real thing. Will you come to see me, Hannah?

Oh, please say yes, because all the other boys will have mummies there and my mummy's in hospital. She can't come out until she's better. Grandma Adele told me that.'

Hannah swallowed the lump in her throat and blinked vigorously to stop the tears forming. So Adele had told him his mummy was in hospital until she got better. No wonder Simon felt committed to the mother of his son. To the little boy she was a living reality. She looked up at Simon, her eyes questioning whether it would be a good idea for her to be seen at the school with his son. Supposing she saw Staff Nurse Carson? How would she explain her reason for being there?

'What do you think, Simon?' There was no need for her to spell it out to him.

'You'd better not disappoint Michael,' he said quietly. His son's welfare came before anything else to him in this situation. 'I'll arrange for you to have a half-day tomorrow. We'll call it personal business.'

She saw the real tenderness in his eyes as she replied, 'I'd love to go.'

'Yippee!' Michael flung his arms around her neck and gave her a big, childish hug. 'And will you stay on for the orange juice and biscuits?'

Hannah agreed that she would as the three of them went into the house.

Mrs Rainer greeted her like a long-lost friend.

'Been too busy to come out and see us, I hear,' she said, putting Hannah's gabardine raincoat in the hall cupboard.

She didn't turn round but Hannah could tell from her tone of voice that she wasn't taken in by the excuses

Simon had been giving over the last two months.

Supper was home-made chicken and leek soup, followed by steak and kidney pie. Michael sampled a little of each before his eyes started to droop.

'Time for bed, Michael,' Simon said, getting up from the table and putting his son over his shoulder.

'Hannah, you come too,' the little boy said sleepily.

Hannah pushed back her chair and followed them up the stairs.

The pink room was now blue and yellow she noticed as she waited for Simon to finish helping Michael brush his teeth in the bathroom, and a bedside lamp decorated with pictures of Postman Pat cast a warm, cosy glow over the room. Michael's duvet-cover was decorated with a selection of dinosaurs and there was a matching pillow. Hannah smiled. She couldn't imagine laying her head down on a brontosaurus and managing to go to sleep, but no doubt the little boy was happy with it.

Simon brought Michael in and put him into bed. The little boy's eyelids drooped further, but he struggled to stay awake.

'Goodnight, Michael.' Hannah bent down and kissed his forehead.

The little arms came up and tiny hands grasped the back of her neck. She swallowed as she remembered that by Christmas this little boy would be three thousand miles away—and so would his daddy.

She went out hurriedly, down the stairs and back into the dining-room, where Mrs Rainer was clearing away the supper things.

'I'll bring your coffee into the sitting-room. Go along in there. I've just made up the fire.'

'I don't think I've time for coffee,' Hannah said. 'I ought to get back to hospital.'

'Nonsense,' Simon said, coming in through the door. 'Another few minutes won't make much difference.'

'A few minutes,' she repeated firmly, not trusting herself to stay longer in this house of too many memories.

As they drank their coffee by the fire she could hear Mrs Rainer working in the kitchen. She hadn't used the ploy of going over to her sister tonight. She'd obviously decided that the relationship between Simon and herself had to remain platonic, so her match-making efforts would be useless.

'Thanks for saying you'll go to Michael's nativity play. It means such a lot to him,' Simon said as he threw another log on the blazing fire. 'He seems extremely fond of you.'

'I'm very fond of him,' she said quietly. 'I wish I'd been able to see more of him. . .while he was here.'

'But you were too busy,' Simon said, with a wry smile.

'So they tell me. And by Christmas you'll both be miles away from here.'

'I'll only be gone a week. Just long enough to take Michael back to Adele.'

'How can you bear to part with him?'

He frowned. 'I find it harder every time I see him. I'm seriously contemplating taking a job in the States so that I can be near him.'

He turned tormented eyes upon her to watch her reaction.

She held her breath, unable to imagine life without

Simon. She'd heard the deeply troubled huskiness in his voice and wanted to reach out to comfort him. But she held back, not trusting her emotions to let her limit herself to comfort. She would want to lose herself in his arms, to experience some of the excitement she'd known when she'd spent the whole night here in this house with him.

She stood up. 'I must go, Simon.' She moved quickly, going out through the door, opening the hall cupboard, taking out her coat, not even putting it on in her haste to escape.

But Simon followed her to the car. A full moon lit up the garden. She could see the tender expression on his face as he opened the car door for her.

She climbed in and he bent to kiss her gently on the lips.

'Goodnight, Hannah. Drive carefully.'

She watched him striding away back inside the house as she reversed until the drive was wide enough to go forward. This was how it had to be but the situation was tearing them both apart. And there would be no solution while Felicity was still technically alive.

If only she had the strength to end their relationship completely! Over the last couple of months she'd tried so hard, but it was no good. And tomorrow she was committing herself even further by going to Michael's school.

'Personal business?' Sara Clarkson queried as she joined Hannah at one of the canteen tables at lunchtime the next day. 'Come on, Hannah, tell me where you're going.'

Hannah put down her knife and fork, pushing away

her plate. 'That's all I'm going to tell you. I'm going on personal business.'

'But what if I want to get in touch with you?'

'I'm not on call. Mr Delaware is going to cover for me.'

Sara gave a wry grin. 'I see.'

'No, you don't!' Hannah snapped.

She saw the concern in her colleague's eyes and wished she'd kept her cool.

'Look, I'm sorry, Hannah. I don't know what's going on between you and Simon Delaware, but whatever it is. . .'

'That's exactly right, Sara. You don't know what's going on, so I wish you'd mind your own business.'

There! She felt better now she'd got that off her chest.

'Hannah, I'm sorry. I didn't mean to pry. But I look on you as a friend as well as a colleague; and I've been hurt because you won't tell me anything.'

'Sara, I can't!' Hannah's voice rose.

'I realise that now,' Sara said quietly. 'And I wouldn't have asked all those questions if I'd known it was upsetting you so much. If there's anything I can do. . .'

'Thanks, Sara, but there isn't. . .apart from not asking any more questions.'

Sara gave a wry grin. 'I promise that was my last question. Well, have a nice time, wherever you're going.'

As Hannah hurried away she wished she could confide in Sara. Of all the people in hospital—apart from Simon—this was a colleague she felt she could trust. But the secret wasn't hers to divulge. She was beginning to understand how Simon felt.

She went back to her room and changed into the red woollen dress she'd bought in a dress-shop in Skipton on her half-day last week.

Very Christmassy, she thought as she twirled in front of the mirror. The sort of dress a little boy would like: nice and bright and cheerful. She wanted him to be proud of her. . .

But you're only a substitute for his mum, she told herself quickly as she pulled on her raincoat. Don't get any ideas.

She parked by the river and walked through Cragdale, not wanting to mingle with the crowd of parents grouped around their cars outside the school. Inside, the headmistress was rushing around, greeting the parents, organising extra chairs at the back of the hall. She nodded briefly at Hannah, who smiled and moved on too quickly for conversation. She chose a seat at the back of the hall, near one of the doors, so she could make a quick exit if she saw anyone she knew. But, as far as she remembered, there was no one else living in Cragdale apart from Staff Nurse Ruth Carson.

It was hot and stuffy in the school hall. Hannah removed her gabardine raincoat, folded it, and put it on her lap. The stage curtains were still closed. She glanced at her watch five minutes to go.

A couple of teachers were closing the window curtains to keep out the pale wintry sun and another teacher switched the hall lights on. Hannah felt decidedly vulnerable.

It wasn't until the lights were dimmed that she felt she could relax.

The stage curtains were pulled back and the play began. She smiled as she saw each of the young players coming on to the stage, some of them stumbling over their lines, others needing a prompt. The little girl angels were delightful in the costumes that had been carefully and lovingly sewn by their mothers.

And then Michael appeared. Hannah found she was holding her breath as he flung open the door of the inn and spoke his line without a hitch. He was looking straight out at the audience, and she hoped he could see her tucked away in the corner at the back.

She remembered she'd promised to stay for the orange juice and biscuits. That might be a bit tricky, but she'd cross that bridge when she came to it.

On stage the children were now singing 'Away in a Manger' as they grouped around the crib. She saw one of the mothers move to the side of the stage with a video camera. Oh, God! It was Ruth Carson. Automatically she shrank down in her seat, and stayed there until the final curtain-call, when she took a hasty peep at Michael smiling out from the front row. He was a handsome little boy; he was going to break a few hearts when he got older, she didn't doubt. Just like his father.

The lights went up and the parents chattered to each other, many of them convinced they'd produced future stars of stage and screen.

Hannah was drawn along in the parental crush towards the dining-room, where everyone was to meet up with their offspring and drink the obligatory orange juice and biscuits. The stale smell of school-dinners did nothing to disperse her apprehension.

Oh, bliss! Hannah could see large metal teapots at

one end of the trestle table. That was more her style.

'Yes, please,' she said, accepting a cup and saucer from the teacher who was pouring out.

'I don't think we've met, Mrs er. . .' the teacher said.

Hannah smiled sweetly. 'I don't think we have. Thank you for the tea.'

She moved away, her eyes riveted to the door where the children would appear. The first ones were arriving now, running to their parents.

'Was I good?'

'Did you like it?'

Hannah listened to the shrieks of excitement, and then she saw Michael coming in. He hesitated at the door, his eyes scanning the room. She went across to him and his little face lit up with delight.

'Hannah!'

She bent down, and the little arms went round her neck.

'You were wonderful, Michael!'

'Was I really? It was lovely up there, but I couldn't see you for the lights shining in my face. I thought you might have forgotten and. . .'

'I wouldn't have forgotten anything so important, Michael,' she said quickly. 'Let's get you some orange juice and biscuits. You must be thirsty.'

'It's Dr Morgan, isn't it?'

Hannah froze as she turned around from the orange juice table, steadying Michael's plastic cup with one hand as she looked at Ruth Carson.

'I didn't know you were involved with this school,' the staff nurse said. 'Oh, you're with Michael Delaware, I see. Well, that explains it.'

'Mr Delaware couldn't come, so he asked me to take

his place,' Hannah answered in a bland tone.

'Well, he certainly makes use of you, doesn't he? Over and above the bounds of duty, I would say. But I suppose if your wife can't be here, the next best thing is to delegate it to your registrar.'

Hannah bent down to hold Michael's drink while he ate his biscuit. She didn't trust herself to reply. Anything she said would be repeated back in hospital and would only cause Simon more anguish. There was an old Yorkshire saying she'd picked up: least said, soonest mended. That was very true.

'Parents may take their children home now if they wish,' called the headmistress, clapping her hands together to gain attention.

Hannah took hold of Michael's hand, aware that Ruth Carson, still hoping for the chance to gossip, was hovering nearby. Michael's orange juice was all gone, the biscuit in his other hand half eaten. They could escape!

'Must dash,' she said to the staff nurse. 'Bye.'

They were out of the door, into the fresh, crisp air. She walked briskly to her car, Michael chattering happily beside her.

She accepted another cup of tea from Mrs Rainer when they got home, drinking it beside the log fire before reading Michael a story from his new dinosaur book.

'You'll stay for supper, won't you?' Mrs Rainer said, coming in to put another log on the fire.

'Please, please!' Michael said, his eyes dancing with excitement.

'Mr Delaware won't be in until late and I know you've got a half-day,' Mrs Rainer said with a smile.

That was true. Simon was covering for her—he wouldn't leave until she arrived back. Their paths wouldn't cross.

'Yes, I'd love to,' she said.

'I thought we might all have an early supper in the kitchen,' Mrs Rainer said. 'Then Michael can go to bed at his usual time. He must be exhausted after the long day he's had.'

Hannah agreed that that would be a good idea. She was glad that Mrs Rainer was so good at looking after Michael but her heart sank as she remembered that in such a short time he would be leaving here, with no set date when he would return.

They had roast chicken followed by yoghurt and honey in the kitchen, sitting at the scrubbed wooden table beside the iron range fireplace. Hannah moved to the old wooden rocking-chair by the kitchen fire when they had finished and Michael climbed on to her lap, clutching his storybook. As he searched for the story he'd chosen he suddenly looked up at her and said, 'If Mummy dies, will you be my mummy?'

She looked up to see Mrs Rainer watching her. What a heart rending question, and how on earth could she answer it?

Mrs Rainer moved towards them and patted Michael's head.

'But you live in America, Michael, and Hannah has to work in her hospital over here. A lot of patients depend on her,' the housekeeper said gently.

Hannah knew it was an inadequate answer, but she couldn't think of anything further to say that would ease the situation. She didn't want to have to lie to Michael.

He seemed to have accepted the explanation as he began, once again, to turn the pages of his book. She looked down at the story he'd chosen and began reading.

Halfway through she sensed a change in Michael's breathing. Looking down at the little boy, she saw he was almost asleep.

She managed to keep him awake long enough to brush his teeth and climb into his pyjamas, before his eyes closed as his head touched the dinosaur pillow.

'Night-night, Hannah, see you soon,' he whispered.

She certainly hoped so as she kissed him gently on the cheek.

Mrs Rainer waved her off from the front door and as Hannah drove away she felt relieved that the housekeeper had stopped asking questions. She must have realised that Hannah and Simon faced an impossible situation.

Back in hospital she went to the porter's desk and asked them to relay a message to Mr Delaware.

'Tell him I'm back, so I'm on call now.'

She didn't trust herself to see him in person. She went back to her room, took off the red dress, and lay down on her bed. With any luck she might get a full night's sleep. . .

The phone was ringing.

'Hello?'

'Hannah?'

She drew in her breath at the sound of Simon's voice.

'How was it—the nativity?'

'It was wonderful. Michael was excellent. Such talent!'

'I suppose that's what all the parents say about their kids.'

She heard the laughter bubbling to the surface in his voice.

'But I'm not a parent,' she said quietly.

'No.' He paused. 'Thank you for taking over.'

'Staff Nurse Carson was there. She gave me the third degree, but I was totally non-commital.'

'Thanks. There'll be more speculation when I take Michael back to the States the week before Christmas. Do you think you can handle it?'

She hesitated. She would be as reticent as Simon. That wouldn't be a problem. It would be the awful gap in her life that she would find so hard.

'Of course I can handle it,' she said, with a confidence she didn't feel. 'Goodnight, Simon.'

'Goodnight.'

It seemed only minutes later. She was in the middle of a deep sleep when the shrilling of the phone woke her again. Wearily she reached out.

'Simon? What do you want? It's two a.m.'

'I've just had a call from the States. Adele was hysterical. Something's happened over there but she wouldn't tell me what over the phone. She said if I didn't want to lose my claim on Michael I had to bring him over at once. I don't know how long I'll be. There's a flight from Manchester at six.'

'But what's happened?'

'I've no idea. Adele was under sedation when I called back. Her husband Tom wouldn't tell me anything, except that I must bring Michael over and be prepared to stay for several weeks.'

She remained silent, stunned by the unpleasant turn of events. Her head buzzed with inconsequential thoughts—she wouldn't see Simon over Christmas; she remembered him saying he'd been seriously thinking about returning to the States for good. It was becoming harder and harder for him to cope with separation from his son.

'Are you still there, Hannah? I have to go. I'll call you when I have any news. Goodbye.'

She put the phone down and buried her head in the pillow to stifle her sobs. For a few indulgent moments she allowed her emotions to take control, before she grabbed a tissue from the bedside table and dried her eyes.

Simon has a family crisis, she told herself. This will happen from time to time. He's totally committed to his son and will always put him first. So you've got to accept the fact that he will soon choose to return to the States for good.

CHAPTER TEN

HANNAH was awakened once more, early next morning, by the shrilling of her bedside phone.

She was surprised to hear the voice of Horace Dixon, the consultant in charge of the other obstetrics and gynaecology firm on Nightingale. She'd seen him many times on the wards and in Outpatients, but had never met him socially or had a long conversation with him. She had a mental picture of him now as she listened. He was a rotund little man, in his late fifties.

'Horace Dixon here. Sorry to disturb you so early, Dr Morgan, but I've had an urgent call from Sir Jack Hamilton, the chairman of the Board of Governors. It appears Simon Delaware has had to go back to America again. Some kind of family problem, I gather. Anyway, I've been asked to take charge of the Delaware firm until. . . Well, until further notice. There seems to be some doubt about whether Mr Delaware will be returning to his position. I thought I would inform you first that you'll be working for me for the foreseeable future. I'm sure we'll get along fine with the new arrangement, so there's no need to worry, my dear.'

'I'm not worrying, Mr Dixon,' she said evenly. Why was he treating her as if she were an inexperienced schoolgirl? she thought testily. 'Thank you for calling. I expect I'll see you later this morning on Nightingale.'

'It's my day off, my dear. If you need me. my

163

secretary will be able to reach me on the golf course.'

She frowned as she put the phone down. The chairman of the governors phoning Horace Dixon in the middle of the night was an ominous turn of events. What sort of machinations were going on behind Simon's back?

Despondently she lay down, snuggling her head into the pillow once more. It would have been therapeutic if she could have slept till her alarm clock went off at seven. She hadn't been called on to the wards during the night, but the prospect of Simon going back to the States, possibly for good, had ensured that she didn't sleep for more than a couple of hours. She'd tossed and turned as her mind went over all the reasons why Simon might have been called back to America.

Felicity. . . Had something happened to Felicity? Guilt and shame flooded through her as she allowed herself to dwell on the possibility that Felicity's artificial life might have ended. She thought about dear little Michael, still believing his mother would get well. How could she harbour such thoughts when. . .?

The phone again! Wearily she answered. Yes, she would come at once.

Pulling on her clothes, she made her way to Nightingale, where Night Sister was struggling with a blocked intravenous drip. Hannah removed the plaster on the patient's hand and discovered it was the cannula which had come loose.

'If you bring me a sterile intravenous pack, I'll set up another one,' she told Sister.

She was fully awake now as she inserted a fresh

cannula and reassured the patient that all was well. The day staff were arriving for duty and assembling themselves at the nurses' station, the ones who'd had an evening off duty gossiping about the night before. They fell silent as Sister Gregson came through the swing doors.

'We'll have our report in a few minutes,' she told the nurses. 'Make yourselves useful while you're waiting. I want to speak to Dr Morgan, if she can spare me a minute.'

Hannah, alarmed by Sister's severe tone, followed her into her room.

'Do sit down.'

Hannah sat on the edge of a chair and waited.

'I don't know how to put this. You seemed deliberately evasive when I last tried to discuss Mr Delaware with you, when I mentioned the fact that he had a little boy at the same school as Staff Nurse Carson. She telephoned me last night to say she'd seen you at the school, apparently in charge of Mr Delaware's son. So I have to assume you understand more of our consultant's family affairs than the rest of us.'

Hannah remained silent.

'I'm not looking for idle gossip,' the older woman continued, 'but I had a rather disturbing phone call from the chairman of the governors this morning. It appears that Mr Delaware had requested leave of absence for an unspecified period; the reason he gave was family problems. The chairman was understandably annoyed by this second request, coming only weeks after Mr Delaware was urgently called away before. He told me he had no choice but to grant the request, but he's decided to review Mr Delaware's contract with Moortown General. If, however, you could throw any light on the nature of. . .'

'I'm afraid I can't help you, Sister,' Hannah interrupted firmly.

'Not even if it means saving Mr Delaware's position here?'

Hannah swallowed hard. 'I've no doubt that Mr Delaware gave the chairman as much information as he thought was required.'

Sister Gregson pursed her lips. 'The chairman has taken the unusual step of putting Mr Dixon in charge of the Delaware firm until such time as the Board of Governors can find a suitable replacement.'

Hannah stared. 'But Mr Delaware has only requested leave of absence. He certainly didn't envisage being replaced at this stage.'

'I gather that he was less than forthcoming with the chairman, who naturally took exception to this and will be calling for a review of his contract today. May I suggest that you go along to see the chairman and explain what you know of Mr Delaware's unusual background?'

Hannah took a deep breath. 'I'm sorry, Sister. I can't do that.'

'So, you would like me to report back to the chairman that he should go ahead with the review of Mr Delaware's contract?'

Hannah turned her head away. Through the window she could see the dark December sky. Somewhere up there Simon was sitting in a plane, dear little Michael beside him, flying further and further away from her. Going away, possibly forever. . .

'You can tell him what you like, Sister,' she said quietly.

Then she walked briskly out of Sister's office and out through the swing doors.

Staff Nurse Ruth Carson called to her from the desk. 'Dr Morgan. . .' But Hannah ignored her. She doubted it would have anything to do with the professional affairs of Nightingale. More likely another probe into Simon's personal life.

She went down to her consulting-room and sat down at the desk, thinking she would make an early start on the reorganisation of her patients' notes on the computer that she'd been planning for some time.

The door opened and Sara Clarkson walked in, carrying a pile of case-notes.

'My, you're the early bird. Couldn't you sleep, Hannah?'

'Got an early call. Are those all for me?' Hannah said, eyeing the pile.

''Fraid so. My list is just as long, but I'm sharing it with James Dewhirst. I'll help you out if I finish first.'

'Thanks.'

'Have you had any breakfast?' Sara asked in a concerned voice.

'No, I didn't have time, but I'll get something later.'

'You'll have something now,' Sara said firmly. 'Can't have you fainting away mid-morning. Coffee and toast OK?'

Hannah smiled gratefully. 'Yes, please.'

Sara was a good friend who really cared about her. The sort of friend she'd love to confide in, if only the impossible secret were hers to confide.

Sara breezed out, to return two minutes later with a plate of hot buttered toast and a mug of coffee.

'Don't do another thing until you've polished that lot off,' Sara said. 'See you later.'

Hannah was just finishing off the last crumb when her phone rang. It was Casualty Sister.

'We've got one of your patients here, Dr Morgan. Came in a few minutes ago. Shall I send her along? It's Mrs Catherine Benson. She's expecting twins in the New Year, but she's been having a few twinges in the night and you'd told her to come in if that happened.'

Hannah pushed her plate to the back of the desk, immediately alert again.

'Get someone to bring her along in a wheelchair, Sister. I don't want her to have to walk through the hospital.'

While she waited Hannah studied Catherine Benson's notes on her computer. This was one of her patients whose full data she had on disk as well as on paper. She'd been monitoring her carefully ever since that outpatient visit back in October, when Catherine had admitted to being averse to having a Caesarean. Hannah remembered that her patient's first baby had been a Caesarean, performed by Horace Dixon, so Catherine had specifically asked to be a patient on the Delaware firm this time, where the chances of a normal delivery were higher.

'Come in, Catherine,' Hannah said, opening the door wide to admit the porter, pushing the chair, a casualty staff nurse and Catherine's husband.

'This is Mike,' Catherine said. 'I'd like him to be with me if I start having the babies today. I really did have awful twinges in the night, but they seem to have stopped now.'

'I'll take a look and see what's happening,' Hannah said.

The porter and the staff nurse left the room and Mike Benson leaned awkwardly against the wall, twisting his hands together nervously.

'Would you like to stay while I examine Catherine, or would you prefer to nip off for a coffee?' Hannah asked gently.

'I'll go and get a coffee,' the young husband said, flashing Hannah a grateful smile. 'Can I get you something, darling?' he asked his wife.

Catherine gave a short laugh. 'Later, perhaps.'

Her husband went out. Hannah helped her patient on to the examination couch.

'To be honest, Dr Morgan, I'd love a cup of coffee, but Mr Dixon told me last week I'd probably have to have a Caesarean. So if I have to have an anaesthetic I'd better not. . .'

To Hannah's dismay, the young woman started to cry. Hannah bent down and put an arm comfortingly around her patient's shoulder. She'd only just discovered, when checking Catherine's notes, that she'd come into Outpatients last week for an unscheduled appointment and had been seen by Horace Dixon.

'I asked if I could see you last week,' Catherine said, rubbing a hand across her eyes. 'But Mr Dixon said you were in Theatre and anyway it was the Dixon firm outpatients day. He gave me another scan and said one of the twins is a breech, so I'd probably need a Caesarean. What do you think, Dr Morgan?'

Privately, Hannah was thinking that it was a good thing that Horace Dixon was on the golf course! She might have given him a piece of her mind about upsetting her patient like this. With any luck, she might be able to do a normal delivery of these twins before he got back from the nineteenth hole.

'Just relax, Catherine, while I check out what's happening, and then I'll let you know what I think,' Hannah said, running her hands deftly over her patient's taut abdomen.

Yes, she could feel one of the twins, its head engaged well down in Catherine's pelvis, but the other twin was the problem. It was virtually sitting on the first twin, quite definitely in a breech presentation, and would have to be delivered feet-first.

Hannah moved away from the couch as she thought out the best course of action. She remembered what she'd read in Catherine's notes about last week's scan. Both babies were estimated to weigh around six pounds, so they were perfectly viable.

She went back to the couch and checked Catherine's blood pressure, disguising her concern when she saw how high it was.

Decisions! Decisions! she thought as she put the sphygmomanometer to one side. Oh, God! If only Simon were here to share this medical problem with her. She could call Sara in for a second opinion, but her junior registrar was not yet as experienced as she was.

Her mind raced ahead, and suddenly she saw clearly what she should do. In view of Catherine's high blood pressure, the sooner she got these babies out the better. But the breech baby would present problems.

On the other hand, she'd delivered breech babies before. . .but not twins.

So what's the difference? said a cool voice inside her head. You get the first one out, slow down the contractions with a swift injection or an intravenous drip if necessary, and then take your time to make a successful breech presentation delivery.

She checked the babies' heartbeats on the monitoring screen.

'Excellent!' she told the anxious mother-to-be. But she didn't mention that the breech twin was showing signs of distress. And why had the contractions stopped? She had to get those babies out as soon as possible. So, it was either induction or Caesarean. In a split-second decision she chose induction.

'I'm going to get your contractions going again,' she said to her patient.

Catherine smiled. 'Does that mean I'm not going to have a Caesarean?'

Hannah gave her patient a confident smile as she reached for the phone. 'Yes, it does. We'll go straight to the delivery room.'

She phoned Sara. 'Could you leave your outpatient list to James Dewhirst and come and do mine? I'm going to induce a patient and deliver her twins this morning.'

'Of course. I'll be with you in a couple of minutes.'

Hannah got a porter to help transfer Catherine to the delivery room, where she set up the Oxytocin intravenous drip that would get the uterine contractions going again. While she waited for the drug to take effect she gathered together her team. She chose two staff midwives from Nightingale, who were very experi-

enced and totally unflappable. Beryl Frost and Jean
Smithson, both in their mid-thirties, could be relied
upon in any emergency.

Two hours after setting up the IV, Hannah found
that Catherine's contractions were strong enough to
deliver the babies. Staff Nurse Frost swabbed the
patient's vulval area while Hannah put the Entonox
machine, with its pain-relieving mask, beside her
patient.

'You can breathe into the mask when you need some
relief, Catherine,' Hannah said.

'I'm OK, Doctor,' Catherine said, pausing for breath
between bouts of panting as she clutched on to her
husband's hand.

Hannah noticed that although Mike Benson had
been scared at first he was now settling in to his supportive role, and appearing more confident as he sat
beside his wife.

The first baby's head appeared at the top of the
birth canal and Hannah eased it gently out. Then came
the shoulders, and seconds later the slippery body
and legs.

'Here's your first son, Catherine,' Hannah said, placing the baby in her patient's arms as soon as the cord
was cut.

She blotted out the cries of delight coming from the
parents as she checked on the second baby, who was
going to need all her expertise. One little foot was
already appearing.

Hannah took a deep breath. 'Take charge of the first
baby, Nurse Smithson, I'm going to need Catherine's
co-operation. Nurse Frost, hold that little foot, please,'
she added quietly, as she decided it would be useless

to slow down the contractions in view of the fact that the baby was in a terribly awkward position and pushing to get out.

She took hold of the second foot when it appeared, and then came the little buttocks. Here was the testing-point!

'Don't push, Catherine!' Hannah urged as she eased the baby's pelvis to the edge of the birth canal. She breathed a sigh of relief as the rest of the body slithered out in a relatively easy movement.

'Your second son, Catherine,' she said, placing the slippery boy in a dressing-towel and handing him to his overjoyed mother.

Only then, as she watched the ecstatic parents, did she relax. She'd achieved what she'd set out to achieve—relatively normal, as opposed to Caesarean delivery for her patient.

When she'd finished all the routine checks, and satisfied herself that both babies were healthy, she left the final stages to the competent staff nurses.

She decided that later, when she'd checked how Sara had got on with her outpatient list, she would go along to Nightingale and make sure that Catherine and her babies were settling in.

As she walked away from the delivery room, Catherine and Mike's profuse thanks still ringing in her ears, she felt the first pang of sadness that she couldn't share her professional happiness with Simon. While she'd been totally involved with the delivery she'd obliterated all thoughts of him. But now. . .

Simon should have been here with her. They should have taken this case together. Oh, God! She wanted so much to be with him.

The pain of separation was almost physical as she walked down the corridor towards Outpatients, the bland, professional expression on her face masking her inner turmoil.

CHAPTER ELEVEN

Two weeks went by, during which Hannah heard nothing from Simon. She immersed herself in her work, trying not to think about what might be keeping him away.

Catherine Benson was discharged after a few days' postnatal care, during which the twins established good feeding patterns and continued to thrive.

Hannah had decided that it was best to avoid her colleagues in any situation where she might be asked questions. The whole hospital was buzzing with speculation about Simon's disappearance.

'Of course he must have a wife in America,' she overheard one of the theatre nurses saying as she scrubbed up beside Horace Dixon.

'I heard she was ill,' another one said, lowering her voice when she noticed Hannah.

'Any news?' Horace Dixon asked, glancing sideways.

Hannah sighed. It was now common knowledge that she was in on the secret of Simon's background. But she was becoming adept at fielding questions.

'About what?' she asked, holding up her hands for a nurse to slip on her sterile gloves.

'You're very loyal, I'll say that for you,' Horace Dixon said, breathing in as a nurse fixed the Velcro on the back of his green theatre gown. 'That's too tight, Nurse!'

'This is the size you've always worn, sir. You must have expanded.'

'OK, don't rub it in. I get enough nagging about my weight from my wife. Go and get the next size up, there's a good girl. Now, where were we, Dr Morgan? Ah, yes, discussing Simon Delaware.'

He looked around imperiously, his eyes beneath the bushy eyebrows dismissing the two remaining nurses. As soon as they went out he continued.

'You realise, of course, that by not disclosing what you know you've put Simon's job in jeopardy. The Board of Governors have advertised his position. They'll start interviewing in the New Year if he hasn't returned. So why don't you be a good girl and. . .?'

'Mr Dixon, I wish you'd remember I'm a qualified doctor and limit your remarks to professional matters. Now, if you don't mind, we've got a long list of patients to deal with.'

Hannah swept through the swing doors into the theatre and stood trembling with anger beside the table. She breathed deeply and slowly, and gradually her nerves calmed. By the time Horace Dixon arrived in his larger sized gown she was fully in control of herself and capable of being professionally civil with her new boss.

They worked their way through the list: there were a couple of hysterectomies, a bilateral salpingectomy requiring the removal of both Fallopian tubes, and three dilatation and curettages, where fibroids were removed from the lining of the uterus.

She had to admit that Horace Dixon was a good surgeon; during the course of the morning she found herself totally involved with their patients and thoughts of Simon were pushed from her mind.

It was only when she went down to the canteen for lunch that the awful feeling of despondency threatened to overwhelm her again. As she went through the doors the smell of overcooked cabbage assailed her nostrils, and Ruth Carson was standing in the queue in front of her.

Hannah turned round and went straight out again. She couldn't face either the hospital food or the inevitable questioning.

She had a couple of hours free. Time to get away from hospital. A breath of fresh air would do her good.

She made for the car park and climbed into her Fiesta. As soon as she was heading out of the town she began to feel better. As if drawn by a magnet she drove towards Cragdale and made for Simon's house by the river.

Switching off the engine and getting out of the car, she went up to the brass-studded door.

'Dr Morgan. What a lovely surprise. Come in, my dear. Have you had lunch. . .?'

Hannah said she hadn't but that she wasn't hungry. Nonsense! she was told. A girl had got to eat.

Oh, it was so good to be back, she thought as she followed the housekeeper into the kitchen and sank down into the rocking-chair where she'd read Michael a story.

'You look tired.' Mrs Rainer stood looking down at her with concerned eyes. 'And you've lost weight. I've been baking some bread, there's chicken and vegetable soup, and we can finish off with apple pie and custard. I'm so glad you came, because I love cooking but I hate eating by myself.'

At the end of the delicious meal Hannah got up
from the table and returned to the rocking-chair. It
was as if she could get in touch with Simon and Michael
simply by sitting there. And it was so relaxing to be
with someone who didn't ask awkward questions.
There had been a companionable silence throughout
the meal, broken only by inconsequential conversation
about Christmas-shopping and the weather.

Hannah looked across at Mrs Rainer, who had
refused all offers of help with the washing-up, saying
that Hannah had to conserve her energy for her afternoon in hospital. The housekeeper was standing by the
sink, her back towards Hannah.

'Mrs Rainer, have you heard any news from Mr
Delaware?'

Her voice croaked in the middle of the question.

The older woman turned round, wiping her hands
on a teatowel, and walked slowly over to the fireplace.
Sitting down opposite Hannah, she shook her head.

'I was wanting to ask you. . .but I didn't dare. You
must get tired of people asking you questions
about him.'

Hannah swallowed. 'I do. It's hard keeping someone
else's secret. He hasn't contacted me, but I thought
he might have told you when he would be back.'

Mrs Rainer's eyes were troubled. 'I'm not sure he
will be coming back, my dear,' she said slowly. 'He
left instructions that, in the event he shouldn't return,
I was to put the house on the market again.'

Hannah took a deep breath. She had to face up
to the worst thing that could happen. Simon wasn't
coming back.

She stood up, feeling the room spin round for a brief

moment. She took hold of the arm of the familiar rocking-chair—probably the last time she would touch it. She would take her memories with her and never come back.

'Thanks for the lunch, Mrs Rainer. You've been so kind. I'll never forget you.'

'But you must come back and see me again. I hope to stay on here, whatever happens.'

'I'm going to be very busy for a while,' she answered obliquely.

Yes, that was for sure. She would immerse herself in her work. Make sure she didn't have time to think.

Mrs Rainer was waving from the door. Hannah put her hand through the open car window and returned the wave before driving out through the gates.

'Goodbye, dream house,' she whispered.

It was Christmas Eve and there was still no word from Simon. She could tell that the governors were hotting up their search for a successor. There had been a couple of smart, thirty-something doctors wandering around Nightingale a few minutes before, accompanied by Horace Dixon.

Hannah had been introduced as 'our very capable senior registrar'. When she'd enquired as to the exact purpose of their visit, Horace had replied airily, 'Oh, they're just getting the feel of the place,' before moving on and making it quite clear that it was none of her business.

She went into her consulting-room and tore off the calendar date from yesterday. December the twenty-fourth now stared her in the face. There was a picture of a Christmas tree and a couple of jolly children.

I don't feel at all jolly, she thought as she sank down on to her chair and picked up the outpatient list. In fact, she wouldn't mind cancelling Christmas this year. Her mother had been badgering her to go over for Christmas lunch, but she didn't think she could face the questions about her supposedly married lover, so she'd said she would be on duty.

Her phone was ringing. She let it ring. One of the nurses would pick it up outside her room. It rang on.

She picked it up. 'Dr Morgan here.'

'Hannah!'

Her world turned upside-down! She gasped for breath. 'Where are you? Why didn't you phone?'

'I can't talk over the phone. Can you come to the house?'

'I'm just about to start my outpatient list. Honestly, Simon, you've got a nerve! I don't——'

'Cut the lecture,' he broke in. 'I know you're mad at me, but I can explain. Come over this evening. . . Christmas Eve.'

His voice was tender.

'Christmas Eve,' she repeated. 'I'll try.'

'If anyone asks, I haven't called you,' he said firmly.

'But. . .' Rona Phillips came in with some more case-notes. 'Goodbye,' Hannah said, and put the phone down.

She summoned up all her professional expertise to get through the afternoon. Among her list were some patients she'd come to know very well, and that always helped to stimulate her interest.

Valerie Simpson came in for an examination and a scan, looking blooming in her early pregnancy and pushing baby Daniel, now eight months old, in his pushchair. Apparently her relationship with Colin was still going well and they were planning a spring wedding, as soon as Valerie's divorce came through.

Judith Brown, the patient who'd had the removal of an ovarian cyst, arrived halfway through the afternoon, thrilled that her GP had done a pregnancy test which had turned out to be positive.

'You said you thought the cyst might be the reason I hadn't conceived, didn't you, Dr Morgan?'

Hannah nodded. 'I'm glad you didn't waste any time.'

'It's going to be our best Christmas so far,' Judith Brown said, beaming happily. 'Are you going anywhere nice, Doctor?'

Hannah hesitated. 'I'll be working most of the time,' she replied. 'But I'm going out tonight.'

She glanced at her watch. Only another couple of hours. . .

Two hours later she drove down into Cragdale. There had been a slight snowfall during the afternoon and the garden of Simon's house had a thick layer covering the grass. She switched off the engine.

The door opened and Simon came out. He was wearing a red wool sweater; she was wearing her red wool dress.

'Snap!' she said, feeling suddenly shy.

'Great minds think alike,' he said. And then he bent his head and kissed her gently.

She felt as if the pent-up passion inside her would melt the snow, but she reminded herself that she was still annoyed with him. Furious, in fact, that he'd kept her in the dark so long.

'I've had a terrible time trying to keep your secret,' she said. 'So the sooner you tell me what's going on the better.'

'I will, all in good time. But come inside. We'll freeze to death out here.'

'Where's Michael?' she asked as he took her hand and led her inside.

'Upstairs asleep. He's suffering from jet-lag, so I put him down for a snooze.'

He drew her into the kitchen.

'Where's Mrs Rainer?'

'Had to go over to see her sister.'

Hannah smiled. 'Oh, that old chestnut!'

'As soon as I told her you were coming over she announced that she'd promised to spend Christmas Eve with her sister. She'll be back tomorrow to cook the turkey.'

He pulled her against him, but she resisted.

'Tell me what's happening. Why did you have to go away?'

They sat down either side of the fireplace, Hannah in her favourite rocker, Simon in Mrs Rainer's armchair. He picked up the poker and lifted a log, to send flames shooting up towards the chimney. Replacing the poker in the hearth, he looked across at her.

'That night when Adele phoned, she was hysterical. I couldn't get her to explain, and when I called back Tom was deliberately unhelpful and uncommunicative. When I arrived at their house all the blinds were drawn. I knew it had to be something very serious.'

Hannah drew in her breath. 'Oh, God, what had happened? Was it. . .was it Felicity?'

He nodded. 'Tom had disconnected the life-support machine.'

'No!'

'Adele was threatening him with litigation and then to divorce him.'

'And how did you feel. . .about Felicity, I mean?'

'Feel? I didn't feel anything at first. I finished grieving for Felicity five years ago. My feelings for her had died even before the car crash.'

'But why did Tom disconnect the machine?'

'He told me he'd had enough of Adele tormenting herself with a dream that wasn't going to come true. He wanted a whole wife, not half a person. So he went to the hospital, waited until there was no one in the room, and switched off the machine. He told me it didn't take long. . . She didn't suffer—her brain hadn't registered anything for five years. . .'

As his voice trailed away she saw the tears in his eyes. For all his protestations, it had been an unnerving experience.

'Before Adele's doctor sedated her, on the day Felicity died, Adele threatened to call in her lawyer and instruct him to begin a criminal indictment against Tom. For several days this was hanging over his head. She wouldn't listen to him. But I made her listen to me,' he finished quietly. 'I was able to persuade her not to go ahead with it.'

'What did you say?' she asked softly.

'I told her that she'd taken away five years of my life—five years in which I could have lived my life to the full instead of putting up with a half-life while I kept her impossible secret. I told her that Tom was a good man and didn't deserve to have his life ruined as she'd almost ruined mine. As a doctor I had known for five years that there was never any hope that Felicity would come out of her coma, but I'd kept the secret for Michael's sake, so that I could claim my side of the bargain. I'd served my sentence, but I wasn't going to stand by and watch Tom suffer the way I had. Having got that off my chest, I played my trump card. I said, after all the trouble we'd taken to keep Felicity's fate a secret from the Press, did she now want it splashed all over the newspapers?

'When I said that, she started to cry. Tom came in and held her close, and that was it. We parted friends. She's still Michael's grandmother, when all's said and done, and she did a marvellous job of bringing him up, but now he's mine. . . And I'm free.'

She heard the husky tenderness in his voice as he stood up and came across towards her. He gave a wry smile as he bent down on one knee on the thick woollen hearthrug.

'This is what they do in romantic historical films, isn't it? Hannah, will you marry me?'

She gave him an indulgent smile, her heart thumping madly. 'You look so funny down there!'

'Answer the question, woman!'

'I wondered when you'd make an honest woman of me, squire. But seriously, Simon. You're going to have to face the music when you get back to hospital. The Board of Governors want to replace you.'

'They're not replacing me; they're replacing Horace Dixon,' Simon said with a wry grin.

Hannah's eyes widened. 'But I thought. . .I mean, the place has been crawling with hopeful-looking candidates.'

Simon smiled. 'The situation is this: you remember the day of the nativity play, when I had a meeting with the board?'

She nodded.

'Sir Jack Hamilton, the chairman, said they were concerned about the fact that in my contract I'd stipulated the right to return to the States in case of family emergencies. He said that they were shortly going to replace Horace Dixon with a younger man—Horace will be sixty in March. He doesn't want to retire, but the board are going to insist he goes. So, in view of the fact that Horace will soon be retired, Sir Jack wanted me to assure them that they could remove the clause about family emergencies. I said I wanted the clause to remain. He warned me that if I took advantage of it again, he would have to think about replacing me.'

'And shortly afterwards you requested leave of absence again, didn't you?' Hannah breathed, remembering that night more than two weeks ago.

Simon nodded. 'Sir Jack was understandably cool when I phoned him, but he said that if I could return by the beginning of the New Year, and if I would agree to the removal of the family emergency clause in my contract, my position would be secure. He said the board didn't want to lose me but that in the circumstances he would have to suspend me until the New Year.'

Hannah smiled. 'And here you are, back before the New Year and with no further cause to go rushing over to America. Have you rung Sir Jack yet?'

'He's gone to Tenerife for a few days over Christmas. I'll ring him when he gets back. He'll be doubly pleased when I tell him of my impending marriage to his favourite registrar. . . Yes, that's what he called you. He told me that night on the phone that he'd hoped to hear wedding-bells between you and me but that obviously he'd been mistaken, as it looked as if I was a family man already, and he was sorry I'd been misleading you.'

'And you said nothing to put him in the picture?'

'How could I? I was still under oath, as it were. All I shall tell him when I speak to him is that my family commitment no longer stands. That's all he needs to know to remove the clause from my contract.'

'What shall we tell our colleagues?'

'We needn't tell them anything. Let them make up their own stories if it gives them pleasure. Some people enjoy a good gossip. Once we're married, my secret past will soon be forgotten. People have very short memories.'

He walked over to the window. 'Come and look at the snow, Hannah.' He put his arm around her shoulders when she joined him.

Outside, the flakes of snow were illuminated by the lights placed at either side of the drive.

'It's settling. You'd better not drive tonight.'

She smiled. 'I could take a taxi.'

He laughed. 'You could thumb a lift on Santa's sleigh, but you're not going to. We'll see Christmas morning in together.'

He pulled her into his arms and she gave herself up to his long, lingering kiss.

From somewhere up above came the sound of feet scampering along the landing.

'We'll have to wait until Michael is tucked up in

bed,' he whispered. 'Will you help me fill his stocking?'

'Yes, when I've made a phone call to my mum and then to the hospital.'

'Make sure everyone knows you'll be snowed up until Boxing Day,' he said.

She nodded, her heart too full for words, as she listened to the sound of little feet clattering down the stairs.

* * *

Look for Sara's own story in NEVER SAY NEVER, out in September.

MILLS & BOON

Kids & Kisses—where kids and romance go hand in hand.

This summer Mills & Boon brings you Kids & Kisses— a set of titles featuring lovable kids as the stars of the show!

**Look out for
Love Without Measure by Caroline Anderson
in July 1995 (Love on Call series).**

Kids...one of life's joys, one of life's treasures.

Kisses...of warmth, kisses of passion, kisses from mothers and kisses from lovers.

In Kids & Kisses...every story has it all.

MILLS & BOON

Always & Forever

This summer Mills & Boon presents the wedding book of the year—three new full-length wedding romances in one heartwarming volume.

Featuring top selling authors:

Debbie Macomber ♥ Jasmine Cresswell
Bethany Campbell

The perfect summer read!

Available: June 1995   Price: £4.99

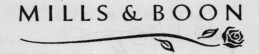

MILLS & BOON

LOVE ON CALL

The books for enjoyment this month are:

IMPOSSIBLE SECRET	Margaret Barker
A PRACTICE MADE PERFECT	Jean Evans
WEDDING SONG	Rebecca Lang
THE DECIDING FACTOR	Laura MacDonald

Treats in store!

Watch next month for the following absorbing stories:

LOVE WITHOUT MEASURE	Caroline Anderson
VERSATILE VET	Mary Bowring
TARRANT'S PRACTICE	Abigail Gordon
DOCTOR'S HONOUR	Marion Lennox

SPRING FLOWERS COMPETITION

How would you like a years supply of Temptation books ABSOLUTELY FREE? Well, you can win them all! All you have to do is complete the word puzzle below and send it in to us by 31st December 1995. The first 5 correct entries picked out of the bag after that date will win a years supply of Temptation books (*four books every month - worth over £90*). What could be easier?

COWSLIP	L	L	E	B	E	U	L	B	Q
BLUEBELL	P	R	I	M	R	O	S	E	A
PRIMROSE	I	D	O	D	Y	U	I	P	R
DAFFODIL	L	O	X	G	O	R	S	E	Y
ANEMONE	S	T	H	R	I	F	T	M	S
DAISY	W	P	I	L	U	T	F	K	I
GORSE	O	E	N	O	M	E	N	A	A
TULIP	C	H	O	N	E	S	T	Y	D
HONESTY									
THRIFT									

PLEASE TURN OVER
FOR DETAILS OF HOW
TO ENTER →

HOW TO ENTER

Hidden in the grid are various British flowers that bloom in the Spring. You'll find the list next to the word puzzle overleaf and they can be read backwards, forwards, up, down, or diagonally. When you find a word, circle it or put a line through it.

After you have completed your word search, don't forget to fill in your name and address in the space provided and pop this page in an envelope (you don't need a stamp) and post it today. Hurry - competition ends 31st December 1995.

Mills & Boon Spring Flower Competition,
FREEPOST,
P.O. Box 344,
Croydon,
Surrey. CR9 9EL

Are you a Reader Service Subscriber?   Yes ❑   No ❑

Ms/Mrs/Miss/Mr _____

Address _____

_____

_____ Postcode _____

One application per household.   **F**

You may be mailed with other offers from other reputable companies as a result of this application. If you would prefer not to receive such offers, please tick box. ❑

COMP395